The

Book

OF

A

Compendium

By

Frank Peak

THIS IS AN APOCALYPSE CONFIDENTIAL BOOK
PUBLISHED BY APOCALYPSE CONFIDENTIAL PRESS
www.apocalypse-confidential.com

First Printing, May 2023

This book is a work of fiction. Names, characters, places and incidents are either the product of the author's imagination or are used fictitiously. Any resemblance to actual events, locales, or persons, living or dead, is entirely coincidental.

Book design by Will Waltz.

ISBN 979-8-9873662-0-2

To Richard Bachman.

But then the demon, much too soon,
Returned one Sunday afternoon.

The Disrespectful Summons - Edward Gorey

CONTENTS

DEMONS

1. Prayer

The handkerchief catches the first drop of blood. Fabric darkens as the spot spreads to fill each delicate fiber. The broken man dabs under his nose, pushes the cloth against the wetness more than is needed, again and again, but a black crust rings the nostril anyway. One wipe across the lip, across the skin between, the line of red where the life ran down. The pink skin is left smudged. He dabs and he wipes but he never comes clean.

The man sitting beside him on the bench is a stranger. The stranger turns pages slowly in a book, a novel written by a surly, long dead Englishman no one remembers. His bowtie is uneven, tied without thought. He takes sporadic bites from a sandwich and the occasional bite of a sliced pickle he places with care on the plastic baggie from which it has been salvaged. His lips move while he reads each line slowly, tasting the flavor of every word. The turn of the page comes only after long gaps of time have gone by. The stranger is lost to his story.

"Nice day."

He folds his handkerchief, half and half again. He doesn't tuck it away, holds it in his lap, one leg folded over the other and clasped hands on top with that neat fold of cloth and blood held somewhere in the middle. The stranger with the book says nothing.

"This park was built in '48."

A grimace, ugly hitching at the lip, as if the lightest attempt at yanking this stranger from his book is an act of violence, an affront to the soul. He blinks and turns the page. The look fades.

Nannies sit on benches. They laugh and share, wanderers basking in a moment of familiarity, a communal experience not of friends or strangers but something in that place between, agents on the job, taskmasters tending, each shepherding its own distinct flock. They trade vapid banalities like baseball cards with always one eye on the children. The kids do not notice their keepers. The herds mingle into one entity, a hive swarming a playground, woodchips and gravel underfoot as the mass plays a schoolyard game with its own internal logic, rules and concepts that make no sense on their own, a contained madness only reasonable in the amoral heart of that hive beast, Child.

The man with the handkerchief looks at his hands.

"I used to come here as a kid. To this park."

Stone wall marks edge, a demarcation separating two worlds. The old and the new. Old men sit at chipped tables, color faded from the wood and from the men, an ancient twisting oak shading the spot so that even the light is not immune to the ashen complexion. They smoke, every one to a man, sucking in and expelling gray clouds like long forgotten cars, boxy hulking beasts with bent fenders and rusting engines and every few minutes a hacking cough or the thunderclap of a backfire. Some talk, leaning over and pointing at some memory as they swap hushed lies. Others play games, a cheap fiber chessboard laid out between them, plastic pieces set up in eternal, futile conquest. One man moves and another does the same. Shrewd eyes narrow.

"En passant," he says as bent fingers wrestle with an off-white pawn.

"Fuck's that mean?"

The second man's gray face reddens as he looks at the yellowing pawn, still held in the air by the other man, the move not yet made.

"Fuck does that mean?" he says again.

A nearby man watches the exchange, laughing. Unwashed curls hang in his face. His lips pull back. He shows teeth as he laughs. His gray t-shirt was once white. A fading image of the Earth is printed in the middle. The caption reads SELL THE PLANET. The gap between each tooth is huge.

The stranger with the book takes a bite of his sandwich without stopping his march along line after line of poorly written prose. He chews slowly, not knowing or maybe not caring that the motion of his jaw is in time to the motion of his eyes, a silent song playing to the beat of his thoughts.

"I pray sometimes."

The stranger with the book wrinkles his noise at the sound of the other man speaking. He doesn't look at him, not directly, just looks around at the park and at the world, taking care to fold the corner of the page in and closing the book. He holds the little bundle of fiction close to his chest as he stands and walks away, half a sandwich left behind on a bench. The other man stares at the sandwich, at the uneven ridges left by the rending of teeth. A line of bright blood appears under one nostril.

"I pray sometimes but I don't think about getting better anymore."

He goes on that way, this broken man, goes on staring at the sad, dead sandwich and chanting to himself, reciting meaningless bids for deliverance, chanting whatever words his heart finds while casually neglecting to specify just to whom it is his prayers are addressed.

2. Grind

The floors are wood. The doors, some of them, are made from the same stuff. The old kind of wood once cut from ancient trees by men with souls. It smells of the finish it was shellacked with an uncountable number of years ago. The building is a downtown shithole, unwanted and unloved by anyone, but the floors are fucking fantastic.

At one end of the hall stands a man. His back is pressed against the wall, balanced there, leaning thin shoulders and head on floral wallpaper while his legs stick out impossibly far, a pose that says boredom, says waiting. He breathes in smoke from some cheap brand cigarette, lets it leak out through the gaps in wide-spaced teeth. One arm dangles out below while the cigarette hand rests on his middle. His dingy shirt reads SELL THE PLANET.

A second man stands outside a door. He picks at his sweater. He watches the door and doesn't smoke. He runs a hand over the stubble of his shaved narrow skull. The sweater is striped, ugly brown and gray. The kind of thing hateful grandmothers knit for grandsons they don't like. This second man is not thin but not fat, not tall but not short. He stares at the door as he speaks.

"We should go in."

The other man exhales smoke and words.

"Go if you like."

"We should go in, Hat."

The first man, Hat, raises a hand toward the door, a halfhearted gesticulation even he doesn't buy. Be my guest.

The roar of something mechanical and enraged bursts behind the door. Saw or drill, jackhammer or earthquake. The second man turns to Hat and points at the door, an unintended imitation of the other man's gesture.

"Iggy, it's Gus' problem. Just wait."

The second man returns to watching the door. This is Iggy. Iggy, named after an irrelevant saint no one remembers. Words begin to form, die, begin again, but they don't quite come out, not yet.

Then they do.

"Doesn't it bother you?"

Hat smokes and says nothing. His eyes look down as he stretches up, leaning only on his head now, his body bowing out from the wall.

"They have horns. In all the stories. Tails and shit."

Hat leaks smoke as he snorts. A laughing dragon or a broken Dodge. He props his cigarette on his lip before he unleashes derision. Purely for effect.

"Think we should chant? Recite some arcane Latin prayer? Something with holy water? Grow up. Tails and shit? Horns?"

The fury of the thing behind the door ramps up. The door rattles in its frame. Doors up and down the hall should open but don't. No one is calling the cops. No one is pounding on walls. No one cares.

Iggy takes a step toward the door.

"I wouldn't."

He takes another step. Hat pops away from the wall, standing up straight. One hand yanks the cigarette from his lip as something shows on his face for the first time. Interest or concern.

"Hey. No."

The sound ceases, cut off in an instant, that roar and its meanings extinguished in the world. The door ends its rattle, becoming once more just a door. There is nothing, a span of dead seconds in which the whole world has gone mute, the sound of the world stolen. Then something, crunching, the familiar sound of plastic playing a chaotic tune for a few seconds, a minute.

More silence.

The door opens.

The bitter waft of thick air. Something like old flowers, sweet mildew. A man stands inside the room that exists just on the other side of those few inches of old wood. Hair slicked with an oil smelling like a long ago decade, a few strands sticking out here and there, a primped and prepared thing come undone. The lenses of his glasses rest in large black frames like that singer from Lubbock. The suit is too big, hangs loose on his emaciated frame. The cut is fine, was fine at one time. Like it had been expensive in another life. Like it was finely tailored, had fit like a dream on whatever unfortunate sap this man had beaten raw and taken it from.

Behind this man are piled several plastic bags.

"Be dears and get the luggage, would you?"

This is Gus. He is a man of faith.

3. Mortification

"Do you offer sanctuary?"

The broken man leans in the doorway, looking around the room for something he doesn't explain in words. He stops his search at times, stops to look into the face of the man in his way.

"The preacher isn't around."

The man has a round face, this man in the way. A round face that looks back without interest, looks only enough to radiate its own sincere vacancy.

"I can wait."

Tables are set up along a hallway wide enough for a truck. Tables line one side, cheap plastic foldouts with students and parishioners sorting through items, a few to a table. Clothes are piled on each, or canned goods, the kinds no one wants, beets or creamed corn. Torn Def Leppard tour shirts from '81 or '83. Spinach.

The broken man passes all this without interest or notice. He watches the opposite wall, passing one open door after another, each open onto the same chamber, a wide room at the center of the building. A temple or theater but without pews, without seating. He stalks the corridor and he looks in on this open emptiness as a drop of blood spills from one nostril.

"Are you okay?"

The round-faced man walks at his side, pointing out mundane items and describing as he goes. This is a table. These are for charity. Those are clothes. His interest in the appearance of blood is perfunctory. The broken man dabs at the spot and doesn't hear the other man.

The broken man turns in at the final door.

The chamber is in transition. Smells of mildew. The carpet is old, dusty. Dents mark where all the things this room should contain once were. Those places, those dents deepen the emptiness of the place. The wrongness. It's been uprooted in places, pulled back and left in rolls that will eventually be removed and replaced with something new and subdued, a gray or muted blue. Folding chairs are left out near the front of the room. A dais stands clear, a block of waxed wood upon which stands a man at times but not now, a suited prose-lytizer or prognosticator, a man of words speaking to the crowds. He is not here. This place is empty.

The broken man takes one of the folding chairs, dragging it with one hand to the middle of the room and sitting where he can look one way or another, taking in the whole room one chunk at a time, as if to view it all at once might overwhelm. He does this but never looks, not up or out. His sight is turned only inward as he sits and waits. Not talking. Not anything.

"The preacher should be back any time."

The man with the round face takes another chair and sits, oblivious of the fact that he is not noticed. He talks, to himself or to no one, leaking inanities onto the world and pointing at the rooms splendor and grace. He points out the stained-glass windows, their intricate designs envisioned by an artist of no consequence, a foreign man of vision remembered by no one.

"Is it preacher or priest?"

The broken man looks straight ahead, his eyes not registering the world. Blood begins to drip from his nose, staining his hand, his cuff, encircling his mouth with a ring of deep red. He no longer dabs with the handkerchief. He no longer notices.

"Is there even a difference?"

The round-faced man asks these questions and others, makes statements that have no bearing or even reasoning, simply lists of words falling onto the lap of the world. He lifts a hand to point at the humble cross along the wall behind the dais, an arrangement of intersecting wood beams brought to the this world from another some years ago, the last vestiges of a temple long since burned to the ground by a wicked and spiteful instrument of punishment.

Blood soaks in. Eyes turn a sickening yellow. Mouth slackens as the broken man leans forward slowly, so slowly, bending double in his chair. Life leaks from his nose, staining everything it touches. The handkerchief falls to the floor with a wet plop. The broken man doesn't fall, only sits, that awkward posture in a cheap folding chair, as the last remains of life leave him forever. The man with the round face points out the intricate tiling that covers the ceiling. They were quarried in some far off mine by monks. He can't remember quite where.

4. Rapture

The dumpster doesn't have a lid. The plastic covering that should be there is missing, just gone. Its dented on one side where something, a car or a vicious kick, pushed in the once flat face. Graffiti runs along the front. Just words: SAVE YOURSELF. Block letters without pizzazz but still something, an underlying style, some inherent artistic spirit that cannot be denied.

Gus sings a quiet song to himself as he pulls one bag after another out from the open trunk and tosses it into the lidless steel trash bin. The swish of liquid in each bag as it makes the move from one place to another is impossible to miss. Each bag hits with a dull thunk that releases stink, old food and worse from the dumpster's innards. When he doesn't know the words he hums.

Gus is in no hurry. The matte black relic rumbles idly, a dull grumpiness it exudes as it waits. 1960 2-door sedan Ford Falcon, spray painted with a lifeless color to downplay the wounds of its hard years. Iggy and Hat sit in the wide backseat. Iggy looks ahead. Hat looks out the window.

A phone rings, shrill and inappropriate in the night. Gus pulls a cell from his pocket and speaks. His voice is muffled, the others can't hear. Iggy looks to Hat. Hat looks out the window.

Conversation goes on, outside, on the phone. Words are heated, then not, then keyed up, then nothing. Quiet for a long time. Iggy leans against the window. Still he hears only his own pulse. Somewhere far off a car alarm starts, then stops.

The trunk slams.

The phone is gone from view when Gus opens the car door. Knowing when the conversation ended is impossible to guess. He looks into the rearview mirror and though his mouth cannot be seen, his eyes smile just the same.

"You won't believe what happened."

Iggy looks into the mirror. Gus looks into Iggy. Hat looks out the window.

———

The landscape is speckled with a thousand churches devoted to a thousand faces of the same indifferent god. Steeples break through the skin of the sky and through the holes pours hot rain. Where one of those temples with one of those steeples only hours ago stood stalwart and proud there is now a ruin, a heap of wet ash that bored men in fire retardant coats look at with bland interest, their services not needed. A solemn vigil takes up residence in place of whatever vain effort would otherwise be underway, whatever doomed attempt to extinguish the already extinguished flames in order to save the ruined remnants of what is by now spent and gone.

Gus' voice carries. He talks with his hands when he talks with his mouth. His grin is filled with unhealthy mirth. He keeps the phone mashed to his ear like he might absorb conversation through feel as much as hearing. Bits of sentences come through glass. Double-paned to keep out the world. A diner, the kind thought to be extinct for decades. Gus paces and talks and waves one hand, the free hand, the one not holding the phone.

Hat can't hear what is being said and doesn't really want to. The gist is clear. He stands on the sidewalk, hands in pockets, a constant shrug. An awning keeps out most of the rain. The name of the diner is stitched in faded thread on the fabric. Earl's. Letters that lean in, like they're on their way to a better place, someplace nice, a fine establishment without chips in the tile floor or the booths with their cigarette burns.

"I don't like him like this."

Hat's words fall out with a discomforting nonchalance. Iggy holds a hand over his own head, trying and failing to hinder the weak spray of droplets getting through. He turns to Hat.

"Like what?"

"Pleased. Enthusiastic. Something's not right."

There is a knock on the glass, a hard rap of knuckles that goes on longer than necessary. They both turn. Gus points at the crowd gathered, at the fire truck doing nothing, at the gawkers gawking. A man with a round face wanders out of the crowd. Tears stream down his face. Inconsolable weeping, the hitching sobs of a child. He doesn't speak and soon he disappears once more.

Iggy turns to Hat. The hand moves with him.

"Who burns down a goddamn church? That's, what is that? That's undignified."

Hat points at the hand above Iggy's head, palm up, awkward fingers clutching at nothing.

"It's just rain."

Iggy turns back to the shifting mass of crowded souls and the burned out husk beyond them. He says nothing.

Snippets of conversation pour out of the circulating crowd. Fragments of shocked platitudes. They go on watching, this crowd, but nothing is happening, nothing is happening. The church is burned. It won't burn again.

The rain starts and stops like it's taking breaths. Hat digs through pockets, one and the other, his hands moving independently of his will until they produce two quarters from a back pocket. He runs a thumb over the dates. A bicentennial and a 1965. The imprinted images are soft from the decades of thumbs running over that same spot.

Gus is there, or has been. The door made no sound as he came out to stand on the sidewalk. He could have been in this spot forever, always. The phone is gone from his hand.

"Go home. Nothing tonight."

Iggy looks at the ruined church and back at Gus, eyes that ask the question his mouth finds the words for a moment later.

"What about this?"

Gus offers unsettling glee in a smile that goes on too long.

"It can only burn once."

He doesn't wait for a response. Long strides take him into and through the crowd that parts as he shoulders through. The hole he creates vanishes almost at once. The sound of the Falcon's engine roaring to life lasts only a moment, then it too moves off, is eaten by the dark and quiet night that exists beyond immediate ruin.

A row of vending machines stocked with out-of-date newspapers lines the diner's exterior wall. Hat picks a machine at random. Each coin drops into a slot with a satisfying clunk. A mechanical whine and the groan of hinges and he yanks out the top one from the stack. The headline foretells a doom that has already come.

He taps Iggy with the paper, still folded in half. Iggy takes it, unfolding the first fold and holding it over his head. The rain falls without notice.

"I don't like him like this," says Hat again.

———

The bolts snap open, one and two. Lights are on as he comes through the door, harsh white overheads and one sad, unnecessary yellow bulb sticking out of a kitschy lamp on a makeshift table of dusty crates. The lights are on because he never turns them off.

Gus stops in the narrow foyer, taking care to throw each bolt, checking each afterward, one and two. The smells of the world seep through the cracks, popcorn and pizza, pot and piss. Sounds come through walls but he doesn't listen, barely registers. The college young and the uninterested old. He checks each bolt again.

A slender hall leads around the apartment's outer edge, a custom layout that alludes to imagined space, allows a walking circuit of the limited area to suggest hidden depths within. The walls are close in width, the space between leaving no room for stretch and making the length of the hall seem impossibly long, an affront to physics. Daily detritus is pulled from pockets, left on foyer table beside envelopes neatly stacked, immediately forgotten. He looks around like there's something he should be remembering, but there is nothing.

The inner wall is segmented by doors that Gus passes before turning at the hall's end. The second hallways is as the first, doors along the way and doors further along before another turn leading back, but he stops halfway along this second hall, turning the shined brass knob on the centermost door. Inside is the single room that makes up the apartment's living space. Dining room, den, kitchen, library. Home. Along the walls are doors leading presumably out to the hall that encircles the inner dwelling. Bolts are held fast on all but the one through which Gus entered. There is no coat rack, no place for these things to go. An aluminum rod hangs from the ceiling with wooden hangars suspended beneath, but these are empty. He lays his too long suit jacket across a weatherworn couch and moves about the business of getting home, nudging items and preparing for another day. There is no television, only racks and racks of books, shelves lined with dry leather tomes that have experienced whole lifetimes without the tender touch of a rag or duster. An entertainment center sits in one corner, an empty fishbowl sitting where a TV should be.

Gus moves about, plodding through the elongated series of pedestrian moments that coalesce as an evening ritual, ending at the center door through which he entered. He throws the bolt, checking it once, and, having does this, he checks again.

———

The town is sloppy wet, raging rivers flowing along gutters lining streets. Iggy jogs, every footfall kicking up a splash of water that soaks his legs. He keeps the newspaper held overhead. The water has soaked through, adding pounds to the sopping mess. It takes both hands to keep it held up.

His jog ends at a walk in front of a house like every other his jog has taken him pass. The windows glow, warm and inviting like memory. Open shades look in on a woman wrapped in cotton shorts and a bland gray t-shirt. She stretches, one foot held in hand, the other reaching out for some imagined bauble in the air in front. There is a name for this, thinks Iggy. This pose is called something. He watches, these thoughts slipping by in non-linear chunks, nuggets of lucidity bundled with a growing redness that swells in his mind and chest. She changes position, other foot in other hand. The mirror image of the first stretch. His breath comes in short gasps.

He moves up the walk.

The bell doesn't ring on the first try. He presses a finger to it a second time, then a third. It rings. He hits it again.

The smell of her sweat is the first thing he notes. The door opens and there it is, that primal stink wafting his way, coming off her in waves, vibrating to the beat of his pulse. A song plays further in the house, something soft and melodic, bells and wind that are almost but not quite swallowed by the rain outside.

"You're late."

She says it with a smile, a joke imbued with a private meaning foreign to the moment.

"I can just go."

She leans in. He does the same. That pungent smell intensifies.

She says, "You won't go."

Her breath is hot. She breathes through her mouth. Long, deep inhaling and exhaling. His breath is faster, manic short breaths as his heart knocks harder in his chest. They breathe each other's air. Hers smells like cinnamon. His is empty, scentless. She speaks again.

"Are you hungry?"

He leans in more, their foreheads almost touching, their lips inches apart. The song ends somewhere in the house, the bells and wind within at last succumbing to the endless crash of rain without. That rain goes on as if it might never end. His lips brush hers as he speaks.

"I could eat."

The door shuts behind as he enters the house. A newspaper sits on the walk, old news soaked through, saturated. Inside the house shades are pulled and the song is replaced with another.

———

Letters spell out a name along a modest sign, a board nailed to the front door, but the word carved in that chipped skin is not what people call the place. The owner is a Russian no one's seen in years. His name is as meaningless as the word on the sign.

Hat smokes in the space between raindrops. He puffs away without notice or care as the sky falls all around. A train rumbles along a track somewhere close by. Buildings shake, windows rattling loose in frames. The train horn lets go a somber moan. It trundles by, its miles of slithering cars only heard and never seen.

Hat looks up, into the sky, into the rain, a taunt to some personal devil, but no one looks back. He takes one last pull off the cigarette and is done.

The cigarette goes out with a fizzle as it hits the wet pavement.

The yellows were once all whites. Tiling that lost its flair long ago. Any sign of youth has been irrevocably stolen from every last inch of the room that Hat crosses, one foot in front of the other. Cracks and wear show a floor uncared for but not unloved. Each footstep snaps on the ground like a minor ballet. Hat lights up another cigarette but forgets it on the bar.

The shelves are lighted and lined with bottles like prizes at a traveling carnival. The waifish bargirl pours two fingers of something bland and cheap. Hat doesn't ask what it is.

"Is he in?"

She cocks her head, puzzled or maybe mocking.

"Who?"

"Penitent Sam."

Her coy demeanor, the slightly pushed out lip and the teasing glimmer of eye, it all goes flat at that.

"He doesn't like when they call him that."

Hat shrugs.

"It's his name."

She brushes a thick fall of curls from her face. Fine bones and pale skin and a moment of nothing. She points at a door. Graffiti and violence scar the wood. Bible verses and genitalia. Phone numbers long since disconnected.

A man sits with a drink at the bar. An oily fluid fills the glass, a muted rainbow swirling on top. He stares into the drink, talking to himself or to no one. Talking to the liquid or to God.

"I was thinking about thinking."

His speech is slow, this man with the glass, syllables dipped in old Southern breeding. Words running together. Louisiana. Maybe Georgia. Maybe fake. Faux genteel.

"That there's a place. A light in us or in our minds or maybe mind, singular, communal, and those times when we're not thinking, in those times what we're doing isn't nothing. We're reaching for that place. Striving, you know? That only in those times do we shrug off the things that we hold or that hold us, and we reach because only in those times can we do so, pushing out hands toward some unknowable light somewhere in the middle of us, in the middle of what we think of as us."

Hat sips his bland rotgut and stares at the man.

"Pay for my drink, Burgess,"

The man snorts at Hat's demand, but this is no answer.

The bathroom door opens under the careful shove of a boot. A man walks through, work boots and old slacks, something that once was pressed and tailored now gone to fray. His age is impossible to guess. Wrinkles and wear that are absent of meaning. A hard 30s or a fresh 60s. He watches the room with hard eyes.

"Burgess, Hat," says the ageless man, sitting down to a glass waiting at the bar. Burgess doesn't look up, only nods at his drink. Hat moves closer to the man but doesn't sit.

"Burgess is buying."

The ageless man looks at his glass.

"Well shit."

He empties it in a single toss, swallowing fast and pointing to the empty. The bargirl tops it off without seeing the men. Hat only sips. Seconds tick by before he talks.

"Gus is working."

The ageless man scoffs and drinks his drink. He speaks only when his skepticism levels off.

"Gus doesn't work. Gus doesn't do anything anymore. He cleans. He doesn't do what you do."

Hat leans on the bar. The lights above shine down in ephemeral hue, a light that is there but fails to touch anything, the world around still held in darkness.

"He's working. He is. Carl called him."

Burgess cuts in with his slow wash of words, that dash of Southern gentility somehow perverted in the sin of this man.

"Gus is a believer. A true man of faith, given up to something more. That's a man who knows the limits of thinking."

The ageless man points to his empty glass but the bargirl does not see. He holds it in his hand like it's been filled. Condensation rims the edge, dripping onto the scarred bar top. He speaks.

"Gus is unwell."

The bargirl steps up, noticing the glass, noticing the way it waits in the air, wanting, shaking, a subtle yearning that doesn't quite demand only because it doesn't have to, because it is, at this moment, filled.

The ageless man goes on.

"These people who do what you do. Some of them are religious. Servants, you know. Looking for exculpation, expiation, whatever. Some are just sick. God's own monsters, out doing the Lord's work. Gus doesn't do this because he thinks it needs done. He does it because he thinks God thinks it needs done."

Burgess sniffs at his own drink and speaks up.

"He means Gus is a psychopath."

Hat waits but there seems to be nothing more.

"That's not advice."

The ageless man's lip curls in mocking glee. He doesn't bother hiding the stark disdain.

"Is that what you want?"

"Something's wrong."

"Something's always wrong."

"But Gus."

The ageless man shrugs and drinks and shrugs again.

"Long as you know. Gus is, Burgess, what's the word?"

Burgess drinks his drink, a fat gulp and gone.

"Unstable."

The ageless man laughs but tries to hide it.

"Good enough."

The door to the world opens. Two men walk through among a gust of clean air. Their names do not matter. These men are not important.

The first man looks at the array of bottles. The top shelf, the middle. He points at one but doesn't speak or order. The other man stands in the doorway, looking across the room at nothing at all.

The bargirl stomps over, a hard frown plastered. She looks mean, bowed up, a practiced model of threat built through generations in the wild.

"I'm not sure what I want."

This man doesn't look at her as he speaks. His eyes stay on the bottles, that one hand pointing around, counting out wishes in the air.

"We can't serve you."

"What?"

"We'll lose our license."

He looks around the room.

"But these guys."

"It's after hours."

The smile appears and spreads on Burgess' face before he speaks to the glass in his hand that's been filled when no one was looking.

"Don't worry, friends. You're not missing out. Drinking has long since lost its sophisticated manner."

If not for that smile he could almost sound sincere.

The men stare at Burgess. Burgess looks at his drink. A stir in the air, something electric. A chemical twist everyone can smell or feel. Something is about to happen.

Hat stands up.

"Hat," says the ageless man.

The two men without names look at Burgess, look at Hat. They do not look at the ageless man.

"Then," says one of the men, but it does not matter which. The two men step back into the night. The door closes behind and the wash of fresh air soon dissipates, pushed back by the harsh tang of sweat and whiskey.

______

The water is running. She's left the bathroom door open but her lithe form is nowhere to be seen. Shower spray speckles a grouted tile floor with impunity. Steam fogs a mirror. The world is lost to that hot fog, clouds swirling first only in that little room, then into the bedroom proper. Moisture beads on every surface. The room sweats.

Iggy sleeps on his back, prone, like a corpse. A cell phone rings on a bedside table but he doesn't hear, doesn't wake. Eyes move behind lids, seeing or remembering.

The cell phone stops ringing. The water stops running. The eyes continue to move, ignorant of events as they happen.

The towel is neatly folded. Some kind of expensive cloth, not cotton, something synthetic. All fluff. She takes it, delicately drying herself a willowy limb at a time. The room moves past her one step at a time. The wet towel leaves a damp spot on the floor. The place she drops that cloth will still be damp tomorrow. The bed contorts under her weight as she sits. The mattress is a sinkhole that traps any who come near. She lies back. The swirl of steam has not yet dissipated. She looks up into it, meandering coils going nowhere, lost in their own wanderings as they slowly diffuse in the spreading air.

She closes her eyes.

The coils are still there, spinning inward into nothing. She watches, in her mind, their pointless trek into nothingness, not hurried but only sliding along as by each moment there is less and less of their existence to measure.

Moisture beads on her skin.

Her legs are smooth, shaven, wet. They are not remarkably long legs, not the legs of a dancer or something that prances on a stage. They are soft, warm things, gorgeous additions to a classical painting brought to life by a playful god. Her arms are splayed, flopped at her sides. Her hair is a halo of disarray. Her vulva looks sad.

The phone begins to ring again. Shrill. The vociferous wail of a much larger, much older phone. She reaches an arm across Iggy's unwaking form and mutes the ringer. If it rings again she does not hear.

———

The lot is a blank slate of concrete. Even the lines on the pavement are gone, taken by the dark or by time. A single light glows in the convenience store, a message to passersby. We're not out of business, we're just not here. Hat looks through the window anyway, the payphone receiver still in hand. The tone goes on bleating in the speaker but he no longer listens. No one will pick up on the other end.

The interior of the convenience store is dusty, uncared for. The place looks deserted. The shelves are lined with packaged items, cookies and band-aids, but the color has faded from their labels. Only that single weak light breaks the otherwise bleak image night brings to the place. The phone goes on crying its meaningless woe. Hat leans back from the window.

The world behind resolves in reflected clarity. The lifeless street, the empty slate lot, the hazy suggestion of sky above, only making itself known in absolute by the start and stop effusion of its hot rains.

He hangs up the phone. Two coins drop into the change slot.

He doesn't check at first, and then he does. Two fingers jammed into the coin slot come away with the dropped change. He rattles them in his palm, lets them jingle. A bicentennial and a 1965. He moves into the empty lot, where soon the dark takes him.

"Make a call?"

The voice comes from nowhere. From the darkness. From anywhere. It has more to say.

"You have the time?"

Hat keeps walking. The darkness moves by slowly. There is someone at his side.

"It's late."

The voice is amused, taunting, mock friendly. Somewhere in the distance, blocks away, a stoplight blinks yellow in case someone comes along.

"You going to that bar over there? Bars don't serve this late."

Hat keeps walking, even paced, one foot in front of the other. He doesn't turn his head to look at the dark spot beside him. He wouldn't recognize the man if he did. The man is unimportant, easily forgettable. The unimportant man smiles, friendly in the dark where no one can see.

Hat squeezes the quarters in his hand. He doesn't see the first swing. He doesn't see what object the unimportant man hits him with in that first swift arc. Maybe he hears the dull thunk the object makes as it connects with the side of his skull, maybe he understands what it means in some dull, far off way, or maybe he doesn't. After the first hit it doesn't matter.

———

The cab smells like pine. Fake pine, the kind of smell that tries but fails to cover up shameless horror. The kind of smell that doesn't smell like actual pine but what pine smells like to the uninformed or unaware, to the dreamer who knows, just knows that this is what pine is like without ever having encountered the smell in nature before or since. The cab smells nothing like pine.

The driver listens to talk radio. He spins a dial and a diode wanders down a line of numbers as static spins, racing past suggestion of voice spitting or sharing or saying nothing. He stops on oldies, something familiar, a song that could be any song from any childhood, a snippet of memory. He hums along and then he doesn't, finger tapping wheel, moving along.

The thing wearing the broken man watches the city go by. It looks out with real interest, lapping up every sight and moment as if each is its own experience saturated with substance and meaning. Its tie is loose and its eyes roll to take it all in. Those eyes are an offense to look at, the sharp lucidity amid yellow sick. The thing lowers the window an inch and another after that. The city noise blooms. Cars and voices somewhere in the dark. A train rumbling unseen.

"The Ronettes."

The thing looks at the back of the cab driver's head. The cab driver looks into the mirror and says it again.

"The Ronettes. You know. Phil Spector?"

A moment passes. He turns down the radio, leaving just the

trickle of song peeking through. The thing speaks.

"What do you do?"

A snort, genuine bemusement. The driver looks into the mirror but the thing is lost in the world on the other side of the window again.

"I drive a cab, man. What."

The thing nods. It sits in silence for minutes as the car moves on. Turns along a route devised by a machine on the dash, a GPS that knows just the way to take things, know just how things should be if only the driver follows along.

"What does life mean to you?"

The thing's voice is casual, conversational as he asks his question. Curious and interested. He does not turn from the window.

"Like what. What is the meaning of life?"

The thing sighs.

"No."

The song on the radio ends. A voice comes on but the sound is too low to hear. Maybe a commercial or a news report, maybe something important that slips by beyond notice or even interest.

"Hey, what? You alright?"

The thing lowers the window as far as it will go. It stops halfway, a locking mechanism inside, some safety measure that matters to someone somewhere. The thing feels the night air on the skin of the dead man it wears, cool gusts brushing by interspersed with the light spray of broken rain as the car moves through an otherwise hot night. It closes its eyes and the city disappears, or the city is still there and for just that moment, a second or two at most, the thing is far away.

"How do you think the world will end?"

———

It looks worse than it is.

Blood covers one side of Hat's face. His shirt is drenched, completely soaked through. Bruises have yet to fully form but they're coming. One ugly gash runs along his forehead doing most of the bleeding. He holds a filthy rag near the spot but not quite on it, accomplishing almost nothing.

His entrance back into the bar brings looks. Burgess points to a glass. The television behind the bar is talking but no one is listening. Water is running in a room behind the bar, a kitchen or prep area. Dishes are shuffled, maybe being washed. The ageless man makes a noise that could be a word.

"Huh."

Declarative, affirming or summing up some fleeting transaction. Hat doesn't immediately respond, only walks to the bar and grabs the glass Burgess pointed to. He drinks it down without noticing or caring what is inside. The ageless man speaks but doesn't look closely at the wounds. He doesn't have to. It's worse than it looks.

"What happened to you?"

"Rain started up again."

"Huh."

"Went to call Iggy."

"Did you call Carl?"

Hat shakes his head. The filthy rag flops into his face, then flops back out.

"Should've called Carl. How'd that work out?"

"He didn't pick up."

The ageless man slaps Hat on the back, not hard but hard enough. Hat's gasp is clear above the din of clattering dishes and droning TV.

"Take heart. Shit happens to good people, too."

———

The pages are brittle. Old. Old in a way that the feeble single syllable struggles to encompass. Gus makes delicate work of each turn of the page, careful of even the slightest bend or stress. He sits, one leg turned over the other, on the room's couch with the book in one hand, the other hand guiding his eyes along the page until it is time to go the next.

The writing is foreign, small, intricate characters scripted in an elegant hand. The language is something old and mixed, an amalgamation of thoughts, thinkers' attempts at capturing a common idea from a range of perspectives. Gus reads along as the same story is told over and over in various ways, never bored or tired. He reads hunched over the book, absorbed.

It's not a noise. Something but not that. An electric hum. A shift in the air. Gus pulls instantly out of the world contained in the arcane language of that dry manuscript. Tiny hairs stand straight, tense. Alert eyes roam the empty room with all its doors. Slowly, slowly, he eases the book shut. He uses no bookmark, doesn't dare crease a page. He won't lose his place. He knows where he is.

A hush in the hall that encircles the room. The whisper of movement or the abrupt silence of the static that was there a moment ago and should be there still. Gus stands from the couch. He places the book with care on a coffee table that is no table, only a trunk with straps and no lock.

A scent creeps in, a tart flavor that sours the tongue. Something sweet and sharp and immersed in its own offense, unashamed and all knowing. Gus crosses the room, confident steps, coming to the center door on the second wall. He throws the locks, one and two. Without gun, without wait, he opens the door.

5. Castaways

The dawn sky is a sheet of gray pulled over the world. The rain has stopped but the sidewalks have not dried and won't anytime soon. Gutters flow with runoff. Potholes and dips are idle pools, crumpled, creased wrappers from cheap candies floating on the surface.

Iggy watches the sidewalk as he moves, each foot flinging out front in flamboyant step. He watches his feet or the windows he passes, watches his reflection matching the progress he makes, eyes not roving out for vain contact but in confirmation of their own existence, that yes, those eyes can still find themselves in the world. I am still here. People move past, early morning phantoms on their way to the day, but they don't look his way and he doesn't see them. Thunder growls or a train rumbles by or both.

The line of storefronts of which the bar is a part is innocuous, a bland series of walls and doors. Some windows are empty, shops closed and moved to better locations, malls or the internet. Hat stands motionless by the curb watching cars go by, watching not individual occurrences of movement but the loose transfer of energy all around. Lights flicker and cars rush and horns honk and doors open and shut as people existing only in this moment appear or disappear forever.

Iggy catches sight of the swollen lump and the jagged gash that runs through Hat's forehead as he finds him there in the reflection of a storefront window.

"Fuck."

Hat turns. Dark blotches mark his face and the patch of shoulder that is exposed by his loose and ratty t-shirt. The bloodstains are gone, washed down a filthy sink, but the shirt is stiff and wrinkled from the effort.

"You need stitches."

Unblinking, unflinching, Hat replies.

"For what."

A declaration, no hint of questioning inflection in the words. He goes on that way, staring into Iggy, and the talk is stricken dead.

They walk in silence for blocks, Hat looking into the empty space before him as he moves through passersby, Iggy looking around, at himself or at nothing. He rubs the stubble on his shaved head. The hand comes away wet, the moist morning air dense and clinging. Swimming as much as walking. Trudging through the moment. A messenger goes by on a bike and a few minutes later so does another or maybe the same one in different clothes. Hat digs through pockets but comes up unsatisfied.

"Do you have any coins?"

Embodied incredulity appears in the wrinkled pulling in of Iggy's face in a full body scoff.

"Who carries coins anymore?"

A card table is set up along the sidewalk, cheap vinyl with folding legs. Magazines line the top. Sports and music books, glossy covers with men in suits or with guitars, women in swimsuits or dripping sweat. Stacks are laid out at the impossibly early hour heedless of rain or time. A man sits on a kiped barstool with the name of whatever establishment from which it was taken stamped along the wood of one leg. The vendor. A stack of newspapers sit untouched on the ground.

"Ask him."

Hat stops by the vendor.

"Do you have any coins?"

The man pulls away from the paperback sitting in his lap with a pout on his drooping face.

"I have change. What are you huntin'?"

"Coins."

The vendor's expression doesn't change. Loose skin hangs low, not a thing of symmetry but a melted sculpture of what might once have been a normal face.

"Not for nothin'."

Hat hands the vendor a dollar.

"Give me two quarters."

The vendor accepts this transaction with a nod, a *These things happen* tilt of assent. Hat looks at the dates before shoving them in a pocket. He gives the same nod as the vendor, a private smile on his face.

They move on, halfhearted steps between drab and faded Art Deco row houses and empty storefronts. Iggy speaks.

"Why?"

"Why what?"

Iggy points at the pocket, at the coins inside. Hat gives that same private smile.

"Providence."

"Ambiguity is not charming."

"Coincidence is a sign of the Divine. You know who said that?"

"I think you're fucking it up. Coincidence is a plebian meddling of the Divine."

Hat waits a beat, then interrupts the sudden disappointed silence left in the wake of Iggy's alteration.

"Well?"

"Well what?"

"You know who said it?" asks Hat with an excessive edge.

"I know the words. I don't know who it came from."

Hat's sigh is loud in the morning world, a burdened release heard above the primordial street noise.

"Someone wise."

Gus' building is a creature in transition. Turn of the twentieth architecture, once a thing of ritz and polish gone to rot, bits here and there refurbished, the block and those that surround purchased by some uptown swell, the entire area to be outfitted with all the amenities and rented to new money looking to slum. Gus' apartment is on the ninth floor. He owns the room, or someone does and he lives there. Gus has never paid any of the coming and going owners. The room has not changed in all its years.

Hat stops out front. He waves a hand, halt. A soft pack of cigarettes come out.

"Before we go up."

His shoulders are hunched against some imagined chill as he lights and smokes, inhaling and exhaling in a few long pulls, a quick cigarette that could have been a leisurely smoke on the blocks of walking. A cop down the block stands by a cab parked with one wheel on the curb. A wreck minutes or hours earlier, low priority, tow truck taking its time to arrive. No one inside the cab. The driver had a stroke or maybe a seizure. Heart attack. The cop chats up a pretty executive in a pencil skirt. She laughs at some unfunny line he throws out. She touches his hand. He leans on the cab.

Hat drops the cigarette half smoked on the pavement, not stamping it out with a shoe but instead leaving it to roll into the gutter where it goes out with a fizzle in the sweeping runoff flow.

The foyer is a cramped space with a suggestion of something beyond, a doorway at one end that opens onto a second room, windowless and empty. The two men do not go through to that wide open space, instead heading for a staircase running up one wall of the tiny room. The stairs have already been redone, worked over and reborn. Some kind of shined stone, a pristine thing that elicits pleasing weak-hearted taps with each step trod upon their polished face.

People pass on the stairs, men carrying tile or beams, tools. On some floors work can be heard, the comforting pound of a hammer hitting home or a radio playing, voices of men talking. The smell of coffee and sawdust.

The ninth floor hallway accepts the two men. They walk without talk, Hat staring ahead, Iggy reading the numbers on doors. There is a pause at Gus' door, a breath. Hat knocks. Iggy looks at Hat.

"You look tired."

The side of Hat's head throbs. His skull is too big for his skin. Bruises groan.

"Makes sense. I haven't slept."

"Well."

Hat knocks again.

They wait as nothing happens. A tension creeps in, the whiff of things gone awry. Iggy reaches to knock but Hat is already turning the knob.

The door swings noiselessly wide. A comment about the unlocked bolt is heard and ignored by Hat as he moves through the empty inner hallway, past the table with its daily leavings, checking door after door, each lock held fast as he passed the first corner. Iggy repeats the impotent message, a feeble hand pointing at a door, the moment dragging him along, one foot in front of the other, deeper into the inner hall.

The middle door of the second hall is shut. Hat stops and stands, waits for Iggy to round the corner before laying a hand on the knob. It turns easily. The door is oiled and silent as it opens onto the main room.

The room exhales the musty breath of a tomb sealed for eons. Nothing is disturbed, all the trappings of its recent master still in their place. Books line shelves, nothing out of true. A tin receptacle stands empty by the door, an umbrella stand without umbrellas. The coat several sizes too large sits where it was last tossed on the back of the room's lived in couch. Hat steps into the room and loosens his gaze, taking in everything at once, searching for something with that unhinged place in the back of his mind, the scanning fingers of ancient understanding reaching out and running along every inch of the room, the unconscious mind looking for what is wrong here.

He finds nothing.

Iggy steps in with caution. No boogeymen are found, no monsters swinging from the rafters, and a tension that should break is instead only heightened. He watches Hat fall onto the couch and continue that loose search of the room, eyes never focusing on any spot but seeing all in snapshot meandering.

"I'm calling Carl," says Iggy.

A slow sinking takes place, Hat folding into the cushions of the impossibly soft couch. He looks at Iggy with genuine perplexity.

"Why?"

"We're supposed to be working."

"Gus is supposed to be working. We're not supposed to be doing anything."

"Where's Gus?"

Hat lets his head fall onto the armrest, an unhurried movement from upright to prone, his feet still on the ground and then one comes up, the second following seconds later. He ignores the question.

"So call Carl if it bothers you."

A book on a table catches his eye. Not a table but a trunk. He opens it but can't read a word and he shuts it without interest. He sets it back down and it is immediately forgotten.

Iggy has his phone out but doesn't dial. Hat sinks further into the couch, his voice coming from somewhere far off.

"It's not our problem."

Iggy, hesitantly at first and then, loosening to the idea, puts his phone away. The sour look on his face has not yet softened.

"I don't know"

Hat's eyes close.

"What don't you know?"

"Where's Gus?"

Hat's words come with one final breath.

"Fuck Gus," he says.

———

The suburban sprawl is empty of warm bodies at this hour. Somewhere in the distance the squared tops of buildings stand out like the capped mountaintops of a symmetrical landscape. The city noise doesn't make it out this far, the racing ants which inhabit those framed husks invisible from here, the whole thing an unmoving haze, a painting plastered on the background of life.

A sprinkler spits out wisps of already warming water, unnecessary jets that add to swollen puddles left by rains. A preset timer left on by an apathetic homeowner turns them on one by one. The thing inside the broken man walks through the path of the jets, pressed slacks' ankles violated by a line of droplets. The thing does not notice, or if it does this does not slow its determined gait. It carries an umbrella in full bloom, but no rain falls and the umbrella keeps out nothing.

A wet ring of brown encircles one nostril where the lasting mark of ruin lingers. The thing dabs at this place with a handkerchief stained with all manner of horror as he moves up the walk to suburban dwelling like all the others. The wedge of cloth disappears into a pocket as he rings the doorbell with one filthy finger. He waits with unflagging patience, not pressing the bell again as time falls off.

The door opens.

"Oh."

A word or a yelp. She heard the bell and thought the person had gone or she didn't and opened for her own reasons, a purpose already flitting away as the day takes a new shade. She looks at him, this thing standing on her stoop, her face a momentary shock soon replaced with a melange of persona, gregarious warmth and the subtle hint of distant dread.

"Are you looking for Iggy?" she asks, but the thing that wears the broken man's skin only shakes its head no.

———

The button doesn't light up when Iggy presses it. He presses it again, not sure if he should wait for an elevator that might not ever come. A diminutive man with a metal toolbox walks by.

"Power's off and on."

Iggy turns and watches the man, who stops outside a door further along. The man's lip curls in silent scorn.

"Or keep waiting. Maybe it'll show up."

The man opens the door and is gone. Iggy turns back to the elevator. He presses the button and turns away, not looking back as he heads for the stairs. He's already in the stairwell when the elevator doors open, without sound, to an empty hall.

The foyer is thick with the wet stink of paint. A man in coveralls talks on a cell phone in a guttural tongue. He gestures with his hands and shrugs a palpable indignation. Iggy passes without making eye contact. The man never looks up from the distant fury he barks into the phone.

The street has changed in minutes. The lifeless cab has been taken away. The cop and his consort are gone. Another man in coveralls runs a roller over the tenement exterior face. Words stenciled on the wall disappear underneath a mute acrylic latex. Ominous works in block letters vanishing from the world. SAVE YOURSELF. The smell of paint drifts without aim along the still wet air.

Iggy follows the damp sidewalk. His gaze follows his body reflected in filthy windows or watches the ground move past below. No one bumps into his passing form, the swelling sea of people slipping past as the day congeals with a flow of humanity. He digs out his phone and dials. He waits far longer than is called for but the silken tongue which belongs at the other end never materializes.

A board nailed to a door marks a change in the endless stream of nondescript stores. The bar. The gasp of thick air washes over Iggy as he enters.

"You just missed Hat if that's why you're here."

Burgess' words come out before his eyes come up from the drink in front of him or the table on which it sits sweating a ring into old wood. His accent has thickened, congealed, still sounds unreal. He sits, his chair facing the door, with a glassy haze in his eyes and a grin that revels in private wickedness. Iggy approaches the table.

"I'm not looking for Hat."

"What are you looking for?"

Iggy lets the question go by, answering whatever he wants.

"Hat's at Gus' place."

The cloud in Burgess' eyes fades. Brow creases as he absorbs this news.

"Why?"

Iggy shrugs.

"Gus wasn't there. We were supposed to meet him. Hat's taking it well."

The ageless man sits at the bar, unmoved in hours or days or unspeakable years. He takes in the exchange with a glance over his shoulder. Iggy doesn't notice. Burgess points to the glass.

"Want one?"

"It's mid morning."

Burgess lets that sit, as if this statement has no relation to his question. The ageless man at the bar speaks up.

"Hat's friend."

Iggy turns.

"Iggy," he says.

"I know your name. Do you like it?"

"Do I like my name?"

"Do you?"

Iggy doesn't examine the question for traps, stumbling blindly forward through words, guided by luck alone.

"I'm used to it."

The man thinks about this or thinks about nothing and simply sits for seconds in silence. When he speaks it could be the same conversation or an entirely new one born of the moment.

"Come here. Sit down."

Iggy complies, docile or curious and utterly immersed.

"How long have you been working?"

Iggy hesitates. The ageless man blows past this with unencumbered disregard.

"Take Hat's cue. Gus isn't your problem. His responsibilities are not yours. You follow?"

Iggy nods.

"Say it."

"I get you."

"Now have a drink."

"I'm not thirsty."

"So."

"It's morning."

"Are you saying no?"

Iggy makes eye contact with himself in a mirror behind the bar as he nods.

"I'm saying no."

The ageless man eyeballs the other man's reflection, mulling something over. Eventually he finds what he's looking for.

"Good."

Iggy turns for the door but his steps are slowed by things unsaid.

The ageless man tosses solemn words at his back.

"He started the Jesuits."

Iggy, slow, not stopping his anemic march for the door, whispers an uncertain question over a shoulder.

"Who?"

"Saint Ignatius. They called them God's marines."

———

Birds squat on roofs of buildings and in trees, on power lines strung between pole after pole that sprout from concrete earth up and down the block. Birds with feathers so black they look wet. Light shimmers and moves over the fine textured surfaces. A few sit on cars, on rusted tops of dying frames or the sleeks hoods of overpriced luxuries. They sit and watch from the boundless depths of indifferent eyes.

The bus is late. The stop is empty but for Iggy and another man. Iggy punches numbers on his phone and listens to apathetic ringing, holding the little block phone to his ear and waiting without reason.

"Schedule's all wrong today."

The man is looking at Iggy. Iggy is looking at the street. He nods like the man's words mean something.

"Might hang up on whoever and call a cab as soon as go on waiting."

The man's shoulders are squared. He doesn't move when he breathes. A bowtie hangs slightly crooked from his neck. The paper bag that dangles loose from the end of one arm is slightly damp at the bottom. Iggy turns to the man with the phone still at his ear as he does. The ringing goes on, listless, endless. The man smiles as rain begins to fall. His teeth are a harsh, fine white.

6. The Morning After

The constant thump of an unseen downpour. Hat wipes sleep from his face and from his eyes and he looks around at the room that finds him but there are no windows, only doors. He sits up, slow and unsure, putting hands to knees, elbows cocked and feet set firm on floor, propping himself like he might come apart if he shows too little care.

The room hasn't changed. Locked doors and stale air. The book waits where he left it on the makeshift table. Many like it line shelves or wait tucked under accumulated trinkets of another man's life. Joints pop as he stands and the rain is a code, a hushed white noise that rises and falls and goes on for so long that it could be a thing imagined, not really there at all.

He turns pages in the book, past indecipherable passages in various hands. His eyes wander but glean nothing save the appreciation of the discipline, that concentrated purpose of lines an art form without name. A finger runs along them, noting the places a pen once knew. He turns another page.

Clippings appear as sporadic episodes. Pedantic musings from defunct papers delighting in all manner of horror. Murder and ruin, bodies found in varying states of disgrace and decay. Pieces from all over filled with forgotten names, grisly crime scene photos of no one important to anyone.

More pages turn.

The back pages are stiff with the glue that holds several pages of laminated photo ID's in place. Unfamiliar faces look out of bland pictures. Addresses from a dozen cities, more, cards from everywhere. Bored, pedestrian eyes. Names that could be anyone.

Hat takes the book with him as he crosses the room. It fits into a shelf vacancy without need to cajole, as if meant to be there, the occupants of that section with bindings more or less alike.

———

Iggy jogs up the walk, past the saturated ground and its sprinklers that could even now be leaking onto the world, undaunted efforts lost to the tumult. He pauses next to a waterlogged newspaper where he left it the night before. He stands and he drips from his fingers and sleeves and wonders if he should try calling one last time.

A stirring inside the house.

He leans in, waiting for the sound to come again, but silence fills its place. The knob turns in his hand, the bolt unthrown and inviting.

Air clings, a humid, grasping thing that runs wet fingers along flesh passing through. Something else, just a hint. Sweet and bitter; old flowers, mildew. He moves dreamlike slow, the driving pound of pulse in temples, through veins, that rapid race of blood while legs drag along achingly unhurried absent reality's grounding.

"Hello?"

Not a sound in response but a hushed change somewhere nearby from one of the house's deeper nooks. The dragging weight of an unnamed dread leans on each moment. He reaches a hand to his head to wipe away something there, a stress that does not fear the ineffective swipe.

"Why?"

Her voice is clouded with prolonged emotion. He looks around for the source but finds nothing, as if she speaks to him from everywhere or from some dark inner place.

"Hello? What's going on?"

She doesn't answer at first, and for a moment he wonders if the voice had been in his head, a punishment for a misspent life. Then she's there and on him, slapping at his shoulders and arms and face with both hands, not scratching, not yet, only forcing a pent up emotion onto the body that has brought this feeling to bear. Letting him know.

She looses a sound over and over, a meaningless chain of words sometimes interspersed with sprays of coherence or with guttural expulsions devoid of meaning but not without purpose, barking harangues that comes wave after wave. He puts up a hand, an arm, a feeble attempt to cover his face.

"Stop."

His voice is shocked and weak but she stops, an abrupt halt that leaves them both standing in awkward pause with arms raised and skin enflamed with moment's pink rage.

He looks her in the eye, a search for something within. A smile or something to recognize, something familiar that is not there. She gulps air and speaks.

"A man came here. To the house."

He waits, still searching her face, her eyes, reaching for the woman he knows.

"What man?"

"What do you do?"

He pulls back as if slapped.

"Iggy, what do you do?"

"I work as a consultant and investigator for a law firm."

"The man said you hurt people."

"Not people."

Pale arms drop to her sides and hang there, shoulders fallen, face slack. Soft lips part slightly. She takes in what she's seeing.

"I don't know what that means, what you mean by that."

His words scramble over hers.

"Stop. What man?"

That dispirited pose doesn't break. The slow rise and fall of a breath is all that moves on her person, a disquieting pattern of sigh after sigh.

"I suppose you want coffee."

She leaves the room without waiting for answer. He follows with a kind of horrified desperation.

The kitchen is cut from a magazine printed in the '50s. Tidy and forlorn, its angles all squared. A coffeemaker gurgles as if bothered by the intrusion as from its underbelly a stream of bitter juice dribbles into the waiting glass bubble beneath. Two cups wait on the cabinet, one empty and one not. She pours the unemptied into the sink and refills both from the maker. The cups, now filled, are placed back in their spots on the countertop, hot air swirling above their rims.

She picks up a cup but doesn't drink or offer it to Iggy. She sets it back down, her eyes on the burned water inside.

"Is it true?"

He moves like he's going to pick up a cup but instead only presses a hand hard on the countertop, leaning with all the weight of some inner horror on the chipped Formica.

"I don't even know how to answer that."

Her lip quivers like a petulant child's. Her voice comes out dipped in barely contained emotion.

"That's meaningless. That doesn't mean anything."

"It's too big to explain."

"You think I won't understand?"

"I think I can't explain in a way that makes it sound sane."

The lip quiver peels to a stony curl of derision.

"Fuck you," she says. "I called the cops."

"Why would you do that?"

"When you got here."

He shakes his head like a dog with an itch.

"No, why?"

"You need to leave now."

He doesn't move and she points without effect at the wall where beyond is the front door. He looks that way, not considering retreat, only seeing what's there.

"This is wrong. What you're doing is wrong."

He says it without feeling, flat words driven with a blunt, emotionless air. She opens a drawer and stares down at its contents, at the jumbled kitchen riffraff inside. She's quiet a long time, seconds playing out between them. When she speaks it's once again shivering words from a frightened child.

"Do you love me?"

Iggy takes another step closer. She tenses, her voice shrill.

"Don't."

More seconds go by before stiff shoulders loosen.

"Iggy, you need to go now."

He doesn't move. She reaches into the drawer.

"Is it true? What he said?"

He looks at her, at the drawer, at the two cups on the counter, steam still dancing lazily in the air, ignorant of the play on stage.

"I don't know how to answer."

The gun that comes out of the drawer with her hand is an unremarkable black thing procured from who knows where. Bought from a store or from the back of a van in a strip mall. Found or stolen or what. He watches it dangle at her side for what seems like hours.

"What are you going to do with that?"

"Do you hurt people?"

He watches the gun sway in place, taunted by an imagined breeze. His mouth is dry when he answers.

"I do a good thing."

She looks at him. Their eyes touch. He tries to move. She leans in.

"I don't even know you," she says as she raises the gun to her temple.

The shot is a clap in the room, a concussive swat at the chest and face and soul. He reaches out, for the gun or for her or for something, some combination he can't say or doesn't know, but it's too late to matter. He does not kneel down or stroke her cheek. He does not weep inconsolably over her as she lays there, blood bright red on the muted tile floor. He stands there, looking at her, not thinking, barely feeling, for seconds, a minute. When he's done, time passed, he bends with calm certainty, and plucks the gun from the floor. His legs carry him into the living room with even, professional steps, the gun placed at a square angle on the coffee table. He takes a seat on the couch with hands spread on knees. Proper posture, back straight. All crisp angles, old fashioned symmetry, a picture out of a magazine but for the gun and a phone left off the hook. He looks at that phone, and sitting that way, elbows arched, back straight, waits to find out if she lied.

———

It's all so tired. The pedestrian clink of ice in a glass and the gush of diaphanous libations that goes on and on. The waves of sweat from flesh, human stink in a hot, compact room. Employees on break from neighborhood insurance hubs or shoe outlets purchase greasy sandwiches or overpriced waters. Some drink warm scotch and lament the ongoing workday. Some dream of quitting but never do.

Burgess leans half over the bar, his somewhat diminutive countenance squared in the bit of mirror there as he straightens a threadbare tie, not silk but something like it, a slick synthetic fabric visibly aged. He tugs at the ends and pulls them apart, straightening and separating and reworking the knot but the length of cloth remains unbalanced.

People move about, oblivious of the man and his tie, ordering drinks with funny names or sandwiches with no names at all, living lives, existing. The pretty young bargirl is absent, replaced with another of the same. Aggressive bob hairdo and tattooed whimsy. She moves fast, pouring drinks and playing out the same prosaic routine as those who have come before.

The tie follows its own path, indifferent to the will of the man orchestrating the tugs behind its awkward posture. Burgess gives a last rueful look into that mirror, genuine remorse staring back at the man standing there, and he is done. A muttered curse is his final lament.

The ageless man seems not to have moved, his position at the bar undisputed. A glass sits at hand, long since gone warm with the day, now waiting only for some hitherto untold signal to be given or moment to occur.

"You think Gus is dead."

Burgess says it flatly, an open promulgation, a thought vomited upon the moment before rephrasing.

"You think Gus is dead?'

The ageless man's fingers are splayed on the wooden bar. Old names are carved there, no one important. Those archaic letters run under his fingers, each once jagged and rough but now worn smooth. He pulls a battered cigarette case from some inner pocket. Silver, once nice. Lenin's face is stamped on the cover and words. Communism is Bestunism. He opens it up, takes one out. He doesn't look around as he sets it on his lip. The bargirl stops moving, a telemarketer holding a wad of dollars now gone unserved.

"You can't smoke in here."

The ageless man rises from his stool, a slow venture that brings hard soled work boots to the floor with an oddly dainty tap. The bargirl is still talking.

"It's against the law."

"It's also bad for me," says the ageless man. He takes his glass in hand as he moves toward the door, ignorant of or just not interested in another law he so blithely breaks.

The rain is a menacing thing, malevolent and ubiquitous. The building shelters a few unharried feet from the torrent but even this is not wholly unscathed. Spots appear on sleeves and pant legs, the errant drop on cheek like phantom tears. He lights the cigarette with a battered Zippo. Stars stamped in the metal next to a year now scratched out.

Burgess isn't there and then he is, this dapper faux southerner. His suit is fitted, a nice cut. Muted pinstripes. Functional with a touch of snap. The tie is crooked and defiant.

"Do you even care?"

The ageless man ponders the suggestion, tastes of its meanings. He smokes and watches the rain. The glass in his hand is noticed as if it might have only just appeared in this place. He sets it on the pavement inches from that godless black heaven's deluge and quickly forgets it once more. He watches the rain and does not speak for a long time. And then he does.

"Who is Gus to me? Picture him. Is he anyone? He's a face, a simple grin that hides something ugly. These fiends have always existed. Madmen harnessed by the times in which they live. He was alive during the Crusades. In the Old West he was Law. He's a beast of the day. Even if he's dead he's alive."

He inhales smoke and lets it out, looking at the cigarette in hand, his face fallen, lines cut with earnest regret.

"It doesn't matter," he says, dropping the butt to the ground. The filter sits swelling with rainwater. The glass with its tepid liquor is wholly forgotten. As wayward raindrops impact the surface its contents slowly rise.

———

The keys are on the foyer table. The kitschy lamp has gone dark, burned out. The overhead whites continue to shine in idyllic ignorance. Hat doesn't lock the door behind him as he leaves.

The Falcon is parked a block up, around a corner next to a kid screaming into a phone about a dream, something incoherent and laced with atavistic rage. Neither looks at the other as Hat passes, opening the door, turning the key. The engine rumbles and everything is okay.

He tries calling twice. From a pay phone that should not work but does, wires hanging loose, frayed, mouthpiece barely attached. They are all this way, relics broken and forgotten, no need to repair. He wonders if he might go back to Gus' apartment and look for a phone but he doesn't go and would not find one if he did.

No one answers the two calls to Iggy's home. Hat does not try a third.

He doesn't listen to the radio as he drives. A light burns in the dial and a song plays but he does not hear. His mind circles sharp objects, dangerous places it should not go. He rolls down the window and listens to the demanding sheet of wind and life and rain, a solid sound composed of or conjured from all these things. Empty streets crawl past, the world fleetingly bereft of humanity and he is alone with himself and that inner place toward which he is hopelessly drawn.

Cancerous suburbs grow and replace the visible landscape, sparse at first and then malignant and soon their faceless fronts are all that is seen, each anonymous growth reflected in the next as far as the eye can see, as far as the mind can accept. He parks the Falcon at a curb that runs arrow straight onward toward the end of time. The engine breathes its threatening growl and sighs as he cuts the ignition. The rain is a blow, hot and alien. Hat steps into the street.

Iggy's house. A patrol car sits empty in the driveway. The front door is closed and whatever waits inside the house is held secret, erased from knowing. Lights are on behind curtains. The day lies in shade though the sun is long from set.

A man and a woman stand on the sidewalk opposite, each watching the scene as if something is happening, but nothing moves in the yard or on the street and an awkward absence of sense hovers over their very presence. He holds an umbrella while she stands in the rain. Several feet separate their bodies, his dry and hers not. He does not offer to share the umbrella and she does not ask. They both watch the house for something to fill a void neither of them can name.

Hat lifts a hand to the house.

"You know the guy who lives there?"

The man with the umbrella looks out at the tumult from his sheltered space.

"Just some guy. They were saying he shot the woman, but he ain't here. Cops took him I guess. Before I could get out here. I don't know."

The man returns his gaze to the house, unwilling to miss some imagined event that might come any moment. The woman in the rain doesn't turn as she speaks.

"It's her house. He was just staying with her. Anyway. I was here. I saw them bring her out."

Fine spray of rain comes from certain letters as she speaks, water running down her face, across her lips, an emphasis unintended, maybe unknown even as it happens. Her clothes are drenched. Hair sticks to face like its painted there.

"Did you know them?"

Hat waits for an answer but does not expect one. He flinches at the low sigh of her voice.

"I'd never seen a thing like that before."

A second patrol car moves along the street, slow, stalking an unseen prey or maybe riding out the rain. No lights or emergency rush but a frenetic energy rises at its approach. The car stops at the foot of the driveway, parking but not shutting off. A squawk of radio chatter as the driver's door opens, an ethereal voice blatting numbers or codes, some arcane diatribe that means nothing, a prayer that goes unanswered. A uniformed man with tired eyes steps out. He takes time to look at the few figures swaying in the rain on the other side of the street. Water runs down their faces and it runs down his. He does not wipe his forehead or put on the hat that he's left on the passenger seat. Before this man has vanished, swallowed up by the house, Hat breaks the gaze to move back to the car, any remaining questions abandoned unasked. Nothing is fixed. Nothing is okay.

7. Making the Rounds

Solemn whistling comes from the labyrinthine depths. A haunting tune that wanders in and out of its own course. The owner of the sound does not come into view, is lost somewhere in that complex tangle of hallways. The song lingers in the sterile warren, rising or thinning but never dying away.

The broken man, the thing he contains, this aberration moves in slow stride, a pause at times with hand on wall. Filthy palm leaves prints behind, smudged aboriginal cave art left to be pondered over in baffled analysis by those who come later. His broken, hobbling trek makes its patient way ever more absolutely into the depths of the maze of halls.

No one stops him, it, or even comes along. No sentinel appears, concerned or horrified. If there are cameras they are not watched. If there is an alarm it is not triggered. There should be locks. There should be guards, police in crisp blues. These things should hinder his progress but if they exist they do not show themselves, rendered inert at his deliberate approach.

The cells line one wall along a hall of cold, dense tile like a freezer. A hard bench with sharp corners sits attached to the wall opposite. On this the broken man lowers himself, a precarious undertaking whose success is only assured at its eventual end. He looks into the cell from his seated position, his back bent in awkward arch, the loose skin of a slack face hanging and pulled. Hands on knees, grandfatherly and misleading. That thing inside looks out of milky eyes. A smell of unspeakable sick comes from his mouth and flesh.

"You should not be in this place."

His voice is a shattered thing, dry and rasping. It cuts in and out as it travels down its line of words. The broken man swallows and opens his mouth to speak again but stalls, waits. A noisy breath washes in and out.

"I have nothing to say," says Iggy. He runs a hand across the grit and stubble that runs across the dome of his head. His back is pushed against the wall of his cell. Posture slumped and unmoving. Eyes half-lidded but watchful. Only his mouth moves. "I could smell you. Down the hall, before you came in. I know what you are."

The broken man's lungs rattle, a throaty sound that could be a laugh or could be nothing, phlegm. Smug derision is ever-present in eyes that never close.

"What does life mean to you?"

That croaking voice lets the last word froth as it trails off. He sits, comfortable in the silence that follows. It does not last. These men are not alone.

"I'm gonna die in this place."

The man in the next cell presses against the bars, an onrush of raw want that reaches out in hollow desperation. Bare feet protrude from the bottoms of tailored slacks. His suit is cut from import-ed fabrics, something dark that soaks up any light that touches its unsullied ends, a slick black or profound blue. Crosses are scarred in fading ink on knuckles unmarked by labors or time. Tattoos of religious symbols are suggested in the ends that jut from cuffs un-buttoned, sleeves that ride up. Manicured hands wave their raging impotence at the hall that surrounds.

The broken man animates. Chords stand out in a neck that lacked articulation only a moment before. The loose face tightens. Teeth show in black gums. A hateful lucidity penetrates the clouded gaze, but that intensity does not turn to the barefoot man in the next cell who goes on raving inarticulate fears.

"They brought me. I'm charged with what. I don't know what I'm doing here."

Iggy's worn pose does not change, but his voice is hard as he looses clipped words.

"Shut up. He's got nothing for you."

The other man takes his hands from the bars, those tattooed crosses retreating with him into the cell's core. Sullen arms cross over that pressed suit. He offers a last grave contemplation.

"I was someone."

The broken man makes his way to his feet. His attention remains on Iggy's cell, the harsh intensity of his consideration not diminishing as he speaks in barren rasp.

"A man stands in a field during a storm. A fiend with only darkness in his heart. He screams to Heaven, to one God or many gods. His mind creates unforgivable blasphemy that his mouth gives voice to for any to hear who will listen. He screams until he has no voice. He leaves. Months later on a clear night another man is in this field. He sleeps in this place and his heart is pure. On this clear night he is struck by a bolt of lightning and struck instantly dead. Is this God? Had there been a mistake, or is the Almighty taking out fostered rage on an innocent? Or could it be neither? The indiscriminate happenstance of a disinterested universe. Or none of these things. Some unforeseen answer beyond the scope of us all."

He closes the space between the bars and himself. Leans in close, that violent stink permeating, bringing water to eyes. Strained face, eyes sunken, a limitless vacancy that goes on forever, that gaze impossible to look upon in its complexities.

"You are but a servant, and it is in this place your master has placed you."

His movements are that of an old man as he makes his withdrawal from the hallway lined with cells. He does not look over his shoulder with menacing eyes, only moves in weak step as if some well of potency has been exhausted and soon his form is absorbed by the maze of halls.

The barefoot man stands hugging himself.

"Do you know that man?"

Iggy does not turn or even move. He stares out at the bench where a moment ago sat an unspeakable beast.

"He's no friend to me."

There is no more talk shared and none that would satisfy. The two men stay that way, the barefoot man looking at Iggy, Iggy looking at the bench. The soft shuffle of retreating feet is the only sound for minutes save the intermittent whistle of an unseen stranger.

———

The pouring onslaught attempts and fails to wash the earth clean. Streets are empty, a ghost town drenched, a civilization pulled under and drowned and only towering, vain affronts to long dead gods are left behind to wither in that ebb and flow tide. Lights flicker as electricity crackles in air. Thunder claps so hard it sucks air from lungs. Lost souls come and go, rushing out of the fleeting safety of one shelter and into another, never long for that open mayhem.

The sun moves behind a sheet of cloud. Day's fated transit endures without witness, indifferent to the absence of watching eyes.

A man in rags dances under a canopy. His feet move in an unpracticed jig, light, meaningless steps of something like real joy. A celebration of some gleeful mystery too bloated for words. Moves with an ease, a thing unbound. He holds a cigarette in one outthrust hand but he does not put the thing to his lips and the tip is untouched by fire. No one smokes anymore.

———

Burgess leans on the sink, hands gripping edges. Bacteria growing, disease spreading. The bathroom is a filthy, cramped space. A hollow place filled with damp horrors. The water runs but he does not touch it, does not wash his hands. His face in the mirror is wary and vacant. Eyes are lost in themselves.

The world outside this tiny room goes on, pieces moving one by one. The door between the barroom and the world beyond opens at the same moment as Burgess opens the one between the bathroom and the bar proper. The man who shambles through the door opposite is a broken, ugly thing whose sallow face darts around with unbridled wickedness.

Heads come up. Burgess stops. The fictitious safety of the pocket void at his back offers the inviting suggestion of retreat. The eyes of the room follow that newcomer down into the barroom's dim interior. Behind the broken man the storm continues for long seconds until the door shuts on its hydraulic hinge with a slow mechanical whine, sealing away the dank room and its leery inhabitants.

Seconds stretch as those waiting faces turn down in worry, unsure of themselves and their place. Some look to others, wondering, maybe hoping they will pull a weapon and shatter the moment, while those others only wait and watch, not knowing what will happen, knowing there is no decision to make.

The broken man takes a seat at the bar, not ordering but marveling at the assortment available should he choose to do so. He smiles at the pretty girl with the tattoos behind the bar. She looks away from his face.

The ageless man leans over and speaks quietly. No one in the room can hear. Short words, jagged syllables meant only for one. The broken man turns to the ageless man and nods, that broken face returning words as its slack veined countenance engages in the exchange. The bargirl steps slowly away, one foot in front of the other. An unspoken stress is eased.

Talk goes on between the two men. Ears of the room strain to grasp what they can, but efforts fall flat and the talk is not for them. Burgess is not among these misguided fools. He moves to the toilet when the tension has passed. He gags over the bowl, a horrible and fruitless sound in his gullet. He tries but fails to throw up. He flushes the commode anyway.

———

He walks with shoulders hunched and hands in pockets, Hat does, an inelegant stride that fails to oppose the rain. He meets no one on the streets and he walks with his head down. The sound of that endless splash along sidewalk and world is immense, a noise that encompasses all. The distance between the street where he parks and the door to the bar is a few feet, but his person is soaked the moment the car is shut off and the world has taken him.

He pauses there, drenched and thoughtful. This door is shut to him, barred as he turns the knob. He pushes anyway but this does nothing. He squints as rain gets in his eyes. There is no window to look through and he moves on from some unspoken tragedy.

Other doors are much the same. People are not home, not where they should be. Gathered allies from imagined crises do not come out from hovels where they have always been known to be. As if the storm has overturned some cosmic ruling, something indelible has become unwritten. Hat does not call Carl. He does not call anyone.

A downtown parking garage. The car is parked and locked and he walks two blocks to a modern complex of homes, apartments that look plastic from the outside and smell like fresh paint within. He walks fast, a trail of damp splotches trailing behind along newly carpeted halls. He knocks on a door, quick knuckle raps that lead to waiting. He knocks again and a bolt snaps. The door opens to the length of a chain.

A boyish face looks out through the cracked space made by the chain. Light hair, the head of a doll. He gives off an unpleasant smell, sweet and foul. Wary eyes look Hat over. They take in the bruised face, the swelling and places marked by scab. This man calls himself Honest, but this is not his name. His voice does not hide its mocking.

"That makes sense."

"Let me in, Honest."

"No."

"One of our guys got picked up."

"Don't be coy, Hat. Who and by whom?"

"No one you know."

"I doubt that."

"Iggy. Cops took him in."

Honest blows air, eyes scrunched and annoyed.

"Cops. Cops. Call a lawyer. Or Sam. Call Sam. You don't need me."

"It might not be a work thing."

"What does that mean?"

"Just what I said."

"What did he do?"

"Honest. Focus. Just get me someone who can talk to him for me."

Pause. Somewhere inside the apartment a television plays a sit-com from a bygone era. The dead laugh before a commercial for toothpaste.

"Wait here."

The door shuts and minutes go by. Hat stands in the pool that has gathered at his feet. Hands in pockets, awkward without knowing it. A man passes by the end of the hall, a line in the distance completely absent of features. This indistinct figure steps back, a returning wraith occupying space in that outlying point without reason or want. It stands, watching or just being. Hat returns the look, himself an indefinite line to whatever proprietor holds sway over that inert shade.

"Do you live here?"

Hat flinches from the curious voice at his side. A cheery thing, unconstrained by the learned volume and modulation of quiet, controlled civility. He turns to the child there, a girl of that indeterminable age between birth and adolescence. She balls tiny fists and looks concerned.

"There's a waiting list."

He waits for her to elaborate but she stands defiant, letting the point stay made as was. The stalemate is broken as Honest bursts from the apartment.

"You. Go."

The child glares for only a moment. Tiny feet make no sound as she flees down the hall for an impossibly long time, disappearing around the corner where the indistinct figure had before paused but now is no more.

"You know her?" asks Hat without real interest.

"Don't talk to people in this building. There is something wrong with these people."

The drive is a long one, an hour of aimless circling as Honest points toward destinations half remembered that ultimately fail to materialize. He touches the radio dial until it stops on a rock station. Old songs full of guitar and big hair. Hat speaks.

"Why Sam?"

A reverie broken.

"What?"

"You said call a lawyer or call Sam."

"Yes. I did."

"Okay."

"Don't get inquisitive, Hat. They can ask you to leave for that."

"Who's they?"

"Everywhere you go there is always a they."

The rest of the ride goes by in silence but for the passage of song after song, the same three or four bands making the same tired point over and over until Honest points at a structure enveloped in an unruly thatch of feral trees the car has driven past two or three times already.

"Stop."

Hat brakes hard, unprepared for the sudden change.

"Park anywhere?"

Honest glares with frank offense.

"Are you asking?"

Hat parks at the curb.

The neighborhood is blackened, streetlights burned out or broken here and there so that only patches of luminosity exist among a greater forest of emptiness that plays out in every direction. Somewhere within that sheet of darkness exists more structures, houses and storefronts of another time that have withered and will continue to do so until they crumble away to nothing, their timeless inhabitants standing silent guard until that time arrives and they are permitted to abandon their vigil.

"Step to," says Honest without looking back as a meaningful stride carries him onward, his battered sneakers snapping like taps along the sidewalk that marches ever into the trees. The rain holds its breath. Hat lights a cigarette and follows.

There is no bell on the porch. Honest looks around, visibly shaken. He knocks on a peeling doorframe, thick blows that are swallowed whole by the aged wood. His composure comes back in an onrush of fake friendliness as the door inches open.

The man standing in the open foyer is a forgettable thing, a face that is there only when looked upon. Even in this moment as he hovers in vacant space the tentative lines of his scant features begin to slip from memory. This faceless man does not ask why they've come, already knowing or just not caring. Honest pushes past. The man follows, not looking at Hat, whose muted footsteps resonate dull thuds in an empty hall.

The faceless man leaves them in an inner room. He offers inarticulate musings, maybe telling them to wait or not, hushed mumbling that trails him out, taking its secrets as it goes.

Three men sit at a table in the room, talking amongst themselves, no visible interest in the newcomers. The three play at cards, an unrecognizable bastardization of an old game several lowbred generations removed from poker. Two of the men bet professionally and lose often. The third man is cavalier and has all the money.

The faceless man's return is unseen. He isn't there and then he is, the card game possessing the attentions of all who might have seen the transition take place. He beckons Hat but halts Honest. The babyfaced Honest offers no protest, engrossed in the turn of other men's cards.

Several rooms pass. The last is a dank place, shadows lining every surface, that dark trapping the hard lines of the room in hazy nuance. The faceless man stops at the entry, not entering until Hat does so first.

The plants are dead. Dozens of them, small and large husks dried and ruined in clay pots of cracked and spent hardpan. A sheet of some dense fabric blocks what might be an expansive window that once lit this room. At the room's center is a chair, a simple thing built from wood shaved and worn. The man seated there looks with pupils dilated and lost at nothing, his head lulled to one side. The skin is tight, an elastic sheet of flesh pulled over a shrieking skull. The jaw hangs open in silent scream. Wisps of beard bloom in places where the hair hasn't fallen away from disease or rot. Fat pink tongue moves and rank air comes from that gaping maw. This abomination lives.

The faceless man speaks from somewhere in the dark.

"Go on if you're going to."

For a moment Hat wonders why he has come to this place. All the articulate mouths and duplicitous players that should be here are not. He frames a thought that he does not speak as the man in the chair stirs in abrupt agitation. Blind eyes turn unseeing upon Hat and that paper grin pulls open further still in obscene, mad glee.

"Help is a four-letter word."

The voice that issues from this depleted husk is a rasp, empty of depth, only sour air and an electric scorn. Hat recoils.

"I shouldn't have come here."

The thing in the chair rocks in its seat.

"But you did."

Dead leaves litter the hardwood floor, some crumpled by age or the uncaring tread of booted feet. A forest of ruin marks this place. The thing in the chair goes on smiling, ignorant of the darkness in which it sits.

"You'll have to ask," whispers that malevolent shell. "It's a rule."

Hat steps deeper into the swirling haze of gloom.

"I have a friend."

The thing cuts in.

"He is a man with whom you work. His inspirations are ambiguous in your mind and in your heart. That man is not your friend."

A beat passes. Hat is unsure if he should go on. He is unsure the abomination will let him.

"Um."

"Yes."

"The man I work with. He was arrested today."

The abomination nods, not hurrying the tale along but only soaking it up, reveling in the words.

"I want to know what he wants."

"You want to know if your employers should be informed."

"It's a concern, yeah."

For long seconds there is only the rasp of that ugly breathing thing sucking air into dry lungs, wheezing that air out through split, grinning lips. The pink tongue snakes out, runs along the horror of that mouth. This does nothing. A leaf falls from a dead plant. The thing speaks.

"To be sure, your employers are aware of this mess. What about the underlying factors."

Hat shrugs at the blind creature.

"Means nothing to me."

The abomination nods its thin skull.

"This is the correct answer. I will ask your friend."

That last word is quick, mocking. Hat clambers to form a retort but the thought dies fast as the thing in the chair sits bolt upright. Cords stand out in thin neck and that grin falters, then widens, then is obliterated altogether in a horrible scream filled with wretched terror. Hat backs away in what should be the direction of the door, but his back hits wood and the door has been closed. He looks into the dark. If the faceless man is there he is concealed in all-knowing shade. The eyes in that thing's head move and they see, their pupils hard and sharp and glinting with a light from someplace now, a source existing somewhere in this place glowing only enough to show its presence in those dreadful, haunting orbs. The scream goes on so long, too long, far past the point where breath should choke off that tearing shriek.

He stops for breath, a great sucking intake that foretells a second scream that does not come. Instead it is a wounded sound from deep within the thing's chest that gradually softens to a low, awful moan. This too falls away and Hat is alone with the quiet, the thing appearing to breath but without sound. The eyes with their hard, haunted vision lose their clarity, that alert look losing out to the milk blindness that came before. The grin takes longer, but this too returns.

"He's coming back. It won't be long now."

The voice is close, right at Hat's ear. He turns to see only the outline of the faceless man in the dark at his side, his forgettable features lost completely to the shadows of the room.

The thing in the chair stirs. Breathing gains a faint whine, inaudible but for the weak rattle at the throat's inner chamber. He speaks.

"Don't bother. He's resigned to whatever comes."

Hat pushes off from the wall, standing up straight and trying not to put a hand out to his side to see if the faceless man is still there.

"What did he say?"

"Would a transcript satisfy?" Sarcastic, dismissive. The stink of this man is oppressive. Its offense had unknowingly dissipated, gone for a moment, that absence only noted at its fated return. "He believes himself guilty."

"Is he?"

"How would you like me to answer that?"

"What? With the answer."

"He believes himself guilty."

"You said that."

"That is the answer to your question."

"Stop."

The grin falters at the edges, an annoyance or disappointment showing through the beast's frenzied mirth. His rasp of voice slows, taking on a forlorn tenor.

"Is he guilty? A weight presses upon him that would astonish and disturb. Did he commit a crime? According to whom? By whose law is this man bound? Would your God punish him for what he's done? Would He notice? Did He let it happen? Was it at His behest?"

Hat puts a hand behind him, reaching out without looking. The knob is there and turns. He looks at this shriveled shell rotting away in the dark. He wants to speak but there is nothing to say. It talks to his back as he turns to go.

"What does life mean to you, Hat?"

The door shuts on silent hinges as he retreats down the hall.

Honest is gone and Hat does not care. The absence of the impish dilettante is unsurprising. The card players have changed tacks. The man with the money has fled, and with him his hoarded spoils. The second and third man continue to bet with nothing in front of them, trading back and forth imagined winnings and losses. They swap hollow jests, each betting his life on the turn of a card. Hat leaves the house behind before it is clear to even the players if the joke contains within its folds the suggestion of truth.

Oppressive heat holds the memory of a rain that has for the moment left this place. A clinging humidity, a world in darkness and drenched in sweat. Hat drops one quarter and then another into a parking meter. He reads familiar dates as they disappear in the slot. Time appears on the meter.

The healthy glow of life burns on the other side of picture windows. People eating eggs or drinking coffee, smoking and sharing plebian observations about their day or the weather. Finishing cups and ordering more. Hat goes inside.

Food smells inundate, overwhelm. Grease and salt and hot, bitter concoctions bringing water to palate. Hat orders from a menu without really looking at the choices or the waitress. He eats in silence.

The hole across the street was a church not long ago. Mud ash now stands in odd humps in place of what was. Walls toppled or beams leaning at dramatic angles form abstract shapes in the ruins of that consecrated shelter. A squad car sits nestled against the curb, tires gently pressed out of shape. The cop listens to the radio, a ball game that's run late. The arson investigators have sifted through the mess and left behind only taped off rows and poles to mark their passage. Makeshift flags of a land claim by ambiguous and now absent overlords. They flutter at times or hang limply in puddles.

The door swings open and Honest glides across the room on an air of contentment. He takes a seat at a stool next to Hat as if their meeting has been preordained. Hat swallows something thick, fat and salt and the elegant superiority over a conquered meal.

"You left me there."

Honest shrugs, as if he's unsure of what this could mean.

"Did I?"

"You did."

A menu is plopped with a crisp snap at Honest's front. He looks at the items, carefully reading each one, but he orders nothing. On his t-shirt is the name of some long forgotten rock band. Letters are faded. He speaks.

"Did he tell you what you wanted to hear?"

Hat waits.

"Did you get fixed up?"

Hat speaks, terse and detached.

"Define, 'fixed up.'"

"That's nice. Delightfully stoic. Reminds me of somebody, you know? Dropping nuggets of words laden with meaning, that air of blissful ignorance when behaving far above your station."

"Oh yeah?"

Baiting, but Honest only nods.

"Who? Gus?"

Genuine offense twists Honest's face.

"Good lord, no. You're not the necklace-of-ears, eat-your-enemies type of asshole. You're the Sam type. The Sam type of asshole."

Chewing stops. Hat rejoins.

"Drunk?"

Honest invades Hat's sovereign space, sniffing the air around Hat's face and mouth, mocking or not. An uncomfortable closeness develops. Hat goes on eating, pretending not to listen to the incessant leak of words from Honest's glib face.

"Maybe. Who knows? But the other type? No. Think. Splayed fingers running across the empty side of the bed. A whiff of some scent, a perfume you don't know the name of that someone important to you wore you don't even know when. These things mean something to you. Gus is a man driven, possessed by a devotion to faith. You, you just do a job. The two can't even be compared."

Hat puts down his fork. Egg hangs from prongs.

"It sounds a lot like you're saying I'm likable because I don't believe in what I do."

"I like the way I said it better."

"Maybe Sam's the wiser of the two. Maybe I should get drunk."

Honest smacks Hat once on the back, a loud swat that could pass for a pat. A couple at a nearby table turn, then quickly look away.

"Maybe you should, at that."

———

Hat parks along the street in front of Gus' building. He doesn't bother pushing down the lock. It doesn't occur to him to do so. The workers have all gone home, or to someone's home, to somewhere else, somewhere not here. The paint smell still permeates, suggestive and threatening. If there is a doorman he isn't here.

He moves through the building without thought, the onrush of exhaustion an unexpected friend that is at once met and accepted. Dragged upstairs on legs that don't feel, down hall and through a door that already he's begun to think of as his own. Through that door and another, the middle in the row, the door that always works. The safe door, he thinks in some sleep-addled way. Of the owner he does not think, or if he does it is only in past tense, a suggestion of a person he came in common contact with but did not truly know. A coworker at a job. A job, not a career. He sets his gun on the chest that serves as a makeshift table. The couch is soft and inviting.

There was a moment, during the drive, when he might have veered off, gone back to the bar to sleep in a room upstairs, to wash the stink of the day from pits and crotch among the grime of piss and lemon that overwhelm the one working bathroom while overnighters and degenerate holy men bang on the door or drink their way through the night. Or not. In that moment, that same crossroads that barely registers, he could gun it, push the car onto the freeway and move on to another world and another life, a place where he isn't who he is and he serves no one and nothing, the horror of a lifetime wasted in supplication of an absent God washed away in the roar of a pumping engine drunk on gasoline fire.

Or not.

The option is there, that same meaningful moment open to a thousand possible tomorrows or to the pleasing prospect of none at all, of stomping pedal until it meets floor and spinning the wheel into the ether, into ruin, into an ending that erases all the unthinkable maybes.

Or not.

———

Lights buzz and somewhere the wandering creatures of night create their songs. The scratch of musical legs rubbing together or the whistles and catcalls of unevolved atavists, pests and poetry cutting through the urban hum of electric now. The broken man stands among it all on a curb, a street corner like any other. He stands idle, not swaying or looking at anything out there beyond that place, his place. Stands like he's waiting for a bus or a cab, for something, but he is not waiting, only standing, only existing, continuing the affront that is that one uncomplicated act.

A vagrant appears, a night pedestrian on his way from one point to another. An individual of no consequence. He stops and stands, this vagrant, interested by the apparition that does the very same, the broken man rooted to spot. He takes off a hat to wipe the sweat of the day from a creased brow. The hat he holds in hand, a bowler, dented and out of fashion. He sets it with care back on head, speaks in affable lilt.

"Do you need some help?"

The broken man exhales foul air and turns the yellow ruin of his dead eyes on the vagrant now absent of words. The bruised pale and purple of the broken man's skin stands stark in the light of buzzing streetlamp. Unpleasant to look upon. If this fiend deigns to conjure word in reply, such offerings remain unheard by any living ear.

8. The Body

That sound is not a dream. The slapping smack of open palm on wood, impact after impact, not stopping and starting in broken intervals but only smack, smack, smack, relentless and constant.

"I'm coming," says Hat, not knowing if he will. He blinks and rises, unsure of his surroundings until seconds pass and eyes clear and the room solidifies as both a place and an idea. He rubs his face but this does nothing. He does not know how long he has been asleep. Not long enough.

"I hear you."

He says this to no one and nothing, to himself and not loud enough for even that to matter. The smacking ceases and leaves only silence and the pad of his own bare feet through first the room and then the hall, his boots left somewhere back by the couch or under its skirted edge, somewhere not where they should be. In this way he is vulnerable to some foreign concept, to some unknown danger without shoes, boots, without the hard march of thick soles to center the universe with order and meaning.

His image crosses a hall mirror, a clean sheet of glass, tall but not long. Minimal frame, someone's idea of art. He looks at his face. The bruises hurt less but look worse. He'd forgotten them until just this moment. Their color has spread but the relevance of their pain to his life has already begun to fade. Lost moments that appear and stay or don't. Chance events that happened to another man in another life.

The bolts snap open, one and two. He speaks with numb lips, waking up with each word.

"Can I help you?"

She's familiar as her figure solidifies in his vision. Bargirl, one of many. Waifish and something else, bright eyes and dark curls. Young but old enough to know it.

"Burgess is looking for you."

She says it as she moves, pushing past and into the apartment's hall. He turns and watches her go, helpless to stop her momentum. One slender finger trails along the wall, the unpainted nail making an audible grate on the wood of each door that is passed.

"What's with the doors?"

He doesn't give an answer and she doesn't wait for one as a look is thrown over a shoulder, fleeting and suggestive, for only that moment and then she is gone.

The correct door stands open. He follows her in. She makes a show of picking up objects, examining them for meaning, turning them over and looking for the stories they have to tell. Fingering the dust on books, flipping through things that belong to neither her nor him. Hat doesn't care. He pulls on socks, fits feet into boots. Laces are pulled military tight.

The awkward thud of some object connecting with the shelf to which it is unceremoniously returned. He strains to look but her body blocks view.

"This isn't your place."

He shrugs at her back.

"Does that matter?"

"They said to hurry."

"They could've called."

"You don't have a phone."

"Okay," says Hat. "What's your name?"

She turns around.

"What's yours?"

He laces the other boot while he talks, the string skipping a hole and he has to do it again.

"You probably know mine already."

She laughs.

"How arrogant of you," she says.

"Hat. My name is Hat."

She nods.

"I know."

"Well."

A word, his, hanging there without anchor or purpose. She looks down, looks away. Pensive, something unsaid, something that isn't hers to say. She says it anyway.

"They think they found Gus."

That look deepens, eyes turned down.

"He shot himself."

Hat looks up from the laces of his boots. He doesn't speak until she meets his eyes.

"That makes sense."

———

There is no drama, no feeling. There is a body and a drawer and a man sitting and watching from a lopsided chair behind a desk, one chair wheel just loose enough to throw off the balance of the whole. A paperback lies in his lap, the page saved by a finger. A laminated badge hangs from a lanyard around his neck. Modest decorations; boring name, bland photo of a tired man that could be the wearer. A cigarette sits lit in an ashtray, slowly burning away to nothing, forgotten as he watches Hat read through an ambiguous file open on a computer screen, searching for answers that are not there. He relents without word, takes two steps and leans against closed lockers whose depths hide neglected corpses or vacant space.

Hat speaks. He expects his breath to come out as fog in the cool of the room, but it does not.

"Is it him?"

The other man shrugs.

"How should I know? Aren't you supposed to tell me?"

"What did you tell the cops?"

"They don't care. These things happen."

The face is a ruin. The face is gone. There should be a sheet, something to obscure this offense, but there is not.

"Shotgun's wrong. Gus has this nickel thirty-eight."

The man behind the desk smirks, leans forward.

"That's the only thing wrong with this picture?"

Hat stands that way, leaning and waiting for the decision to be made for him, for someone else to make the call. He mumbles.

"I don't know."

The other man turns the paperback over in his lap, flops open to his page, but he does not look at the words. Seconds pass until finally he speaks.

"Look it, there's not gonna be an investigation. It's him or it's not. If you think somebody gives a shit, they don't. Allow me to divest you of this notion straight away."

The paperback bobs in the air in mock sign of the cross. The bent cover shows a man in coat and hat, a detective wreathed in smoke. Its pages are yellowed with age.

———

He sits there, in that stink of hot, wet leather that permeates the car interior. A classic piece of automotive art carved from steel and rage. He smokes and the windows are down, all of them, each dropped as far as it will go but that smell is unremitting. He sits in it and goes away, looking for something, searching. He raises the cigarette to his lips. A woman walks by. She holds an umbrella though the rains have gone. The sky isn't blue but it is no longer black. The hour is unclear, morning, not early but not busy, not day. Others wear coats or hide under hats. The heat is an aggressive knuckle pushing into the spine, fingers on flesh, a squeezing, kneading thing. No one seems to notice. He breathes smoke as they move past in every direction, forever.

He should call someone. He should call Carl. Carl, that amorphous voice of middle management. He should call Carl, but Carl should have sent someone, a word or an order. A direction. Carl should have called him.

He should call the bar. Penitent Sam will listen and nod, listen and not care. Burgess will laugh or he won't listen at all. Iggy is in jail and Gus may be dead and nothing is happening, nothing has changed. All the world is the same.

Hat should call someone, but he does not. He smokes in the wet leather stink of the car. A woman opens an umbrella as she walks by. It is not raining, but it still might.

The smell of cheap food is abrasive.

"I like bread," says the man with the crosses tattooed on his knuckles. His finely cut suit is stitched with wrinkles. It flops as he waves a half-eaten roll around in fruitless effort to illustrate some point. "These rolls are shit."

He wiggles bare toes, tapping a chaotic beat. Bored, wired, and stuck in this place. Chews bland roll into paste, speaks again without bothering to swallow.

"Is this normal?"

Iggy chews bland meat flavored with too much salt. Memory pops, tastes of childhood flavors, choking down school lunches at age twelve. The food is awful.

"Normal relative to what?"

Roll grease stains slacks as the barefoot man taps the bread on his knee, accentuating words at times or just hammering home a point to himself.

"They move people. To county, you know? The drunks they keep around. The warrant dips? Paying off a ticket on the cheap. You drunk? Paying off a warrant? I'm not drunk. We've been here what. Too long. They don't keep people overnight. This is not normal."

Iggy eats in silence a moment, speaking only when a thought won't be allayed.

"You've been awake too long. Eat your bread." And after a moment, "There's no one else here."

The barefoot man sets down the gnawed remains of his roll. He wipes his hands on his pants without notice. Leans forward, speaks.

"Did you do it?"

"Do what?"

"Look around. Whatever you're here for. What are you here for?"

"A friend of mine died."

"Did you do it?"

Iggy thinks about the question for longer than he needs.

"I deserve to be here."

The barefoot man nods.

"Everybody does," he says, still nodding several seconds too long. Shrewd eyes narrow when Iggy isn't looking. "What are you guilty of?"

Iggy responds, eyes cast down.

"I don't want to talk anymore."

Footfalls can be heard for a long minute before a cop dressed in meticulously sharpened black garb rounds corner, walking in long stride on strapped military boots not shined but darkened in boot-black. He brings in tow a smiling young man with an unimpressive face. The officer nods as he moves past the cells. The young man waves. Paint stains hands otherwise unmarked by the telling lines of work or time. He's placed in the cell just beyond the barefoot man, the candid air of affability he brings not lifting as the bars close around him.

The cop doesn't speak, and soon he is gone.

Lunch comes around for the newcomer, another plate of the same bland mess. He ignores this, pulling a pen from somewhere on his person, a secreted treasure in this desolate hole. He scribbles words on a magazine left behind by someone not seen, long gone, this appropriated periodical extolling the virtues of an automobile already considered at best passe, at worst obsolete. He writes without care for the content already inhabiting this space. His words disappear in dark, appear again in margins. He smiles to himself as he goes.

"Can I have your roll?" says the barefoot man, but if the newcomer hears it does not show.

———

The lunch crowd is soused and not bothering to hide it. Citizens enter and exit with sandwiches in tow, the sharp cut of whiskey on breath as they pass. The others, the regulars that inhabit this hole, they spread an unseemly merriment that infects the outsiders, the neighborhood employees, pedestrians and folks. There is talk in huddled groupings, men in corners whispering sordid tales, spreading rumors. Hat walks among them, not talking but listening. The lunch crowd soaks up the enjoyment without deigning to partake of the dubious frivolities, without knowing what they're missing.

Snippets of talk make rings around the room. Someone is dead. One of them, says someone. One of theirs. A break in the rules, killing without sanction. Murder. Someone's gone off script, avenging in the name of God, fighting the good fight. Gus, says a whisper between leaning conspirators. The talk says Gus did it, Gus killed one on his own. He's broken ranks, they say. No one is saying what makes them think it's him. It makes for a good story. Proof is irrelevant. The story unfolds. Hat stops listening.

"I guess you heard."

Burgess squints against some imagined plight. His words fall flat, hanging there in open space, awkward and ungrounded. He does not clarify their meaning and Hat does not ask.

"Yeah. Yeah, I have," says Hat, though he has not.

"You talked to Carl?"

Hat only shrugs. It's a question he's already been asked. Nothing has changed.

"You should talk to Carl."

"He hasn't called."

Burgess shakes his head.

"No. Go see him."

He waves a hand around at the room, a gesture that fails to signify any one particular thing.

"You believe all this?"

And he does. Hat does. Whatever it is, he accepts it easily with a halfhearted nod, not interested but only acknowledging the fleeting receipt of the inevitable. This small gesture is enough. Burgess is satisfied, or he isn't but he hides it well. He turns and is soon gone, vanished into the hum of the room, and with him his false twang of southern decorum.

Hat looks at the bartender, sees her maybe for the first time. A pretty thing, a little tired in the eyes, but sharp. Mussed hair in hanging curls, a spot of moisture on the upper lip from a drink just taken or maybe just the heat of the day and world. She smiles when she sees him looking. He wonders if she knows what he does for a living.

———

Iggy is awake. He doesn't remember falling asleep. His eyes are still heavy with an dull ache that winds into the seams of his skull. He is alone in this place, in his cell and in this hall. The line of cells has been emptied of its few inhabitants. Of them there is no sign. He looks around, but there is no one to look at. On the floor of not his cell or the next but further down, several over, the one that for a short time housed a young man with a disquieting smile, in that cell sits a magazine, its pages defaced by the hectic scribblings of a devoted hand. The same note over and over. Save yourself.

Iggy cannot see the words written there from where he sits on the hot floor of his cell, doesn't even try, doesn't care. The words are not for him.

———

Evening and a dying sun. Hat manhandles a ring of keys with very few adornments hanging from the loop. One is for the car, the rest don't matter. He should throw them away but hasn't.

"You thought they killed me."

The voice is unfamiliar. Hat turns to the owner of the words, but the face means nothing to him. Pale skin, sickly with veins blue and crawling underneath the surface. Milk eyes look out at nothing.

"I don't know who you are."

"Yes, you do," says the broken man. When he opens his mouth there comes a foul horror, the scent of some unspeakable sin there, ripe and unashamed in every slow breath.

There is danger in this man.

"I'll only keep you a moment. I just want to look at you."

Those empty eyes turn to Hat, stopping there and staying, holding. They look but register nothing, or maybe not. Maybe they see more, see beyond what they should. Those dead eyes fasten themselves to Hat's own and slowly, imperceptibly, the broken man begins to smile.

"What does life mean to you?"

Hat steps away from the broken man. He opens the car door and steps in.

"I don't know you," he says as he slams the door.

———

It's late, almost early. Hours have vanished with all the substance of a fine vapor. Streetlights hum in the distance, their light touching only what it wants.

The steps are old wood, dry and warped with ends that creak under the weight of each footfall. They lead up and onto a wide porch framed by a chipped and peeling railing made from the same rotting lumber. The house is old and the street is empty, no one around for blocks. The interstate runs by somewhere above, only the tops of semis visible over the concrete lip. An underpass wheels back into darkness, and in the other direction is an empty street that may never end.

He knocks and he waits but Hat doesn't see the man watching him through the window until the curtains move. The door opens, first the thick oak behemoth holding in that little world and then the rickety screen door that lies one step closer to the outside.

"You can't come in here."

Carl. Thin, too thin with wires of muscle in arms that lean draped on the frame of the door. He pushes back the hat piled on his head, an old flat cap dented in places, the kind of thing drivers wear in old movies.

Hat takes a step back, inviting Carl into the world.

"We should talk."

Carl's smile broadens as his eyes narrow. He nods when seconds have gone by.

"We can do that."

The screen door smacks the wall and comes back, hanging halfway between open and closed. A spring dangles loose from a hook where it should pull the door closed but is no longer bothered with.

Carl gestures at a tap protruding from the house wall. A rudimentary bar is lined with half-empty bottles and a number of unwashed glasses.

"Something to drink? Whiskey?"

"Just water."

"Water. They still make that?"

Carl turns on the tap, rinses a glass for several seconds. Examines it, rinses again. Hat takes the glass and drinks without comment. Carl pours nothing for himself. He speaks.

"It's a long way out here."

Hat leans against the porch railing, a posture that should say casual but doesn't.

"I want to ask you something."

"Coming out here to do it's not exactly protocol."

"Does it matter?"

Carl doesn't answer. He stands with hands in pockets, his loose gaze hung without care on the dark underpass.

"There's a man out there sometimes. I see him. At night or in the mornings, doesn't matter. Guy in a nice white suit, out there in the dark. Standing under the highway. He never comes closer, never comes up to the house. Just stands out there. Watching."

Hat sips the water before joining the talk.

"We're not normal. People who do what we do."

Carl doesn't turn.

"What's normal?"

An engine rises as a boxy sedan looms. It can be seen from a long way off, its slow approach observed with real interest by the two men as it nears and passes, running lights throwing glow upon the empty walls of the underpass as it rounds the corner and disappears, enveloped in that underworld gloom.

"Sam talks about it sometimes. You know Penitent Sam?"

Unpleasant curl of lip, there and gone.

"I know Sam," says Carl.

"He thinks we're all murderers and psychopaths."

"What do you think?"

"I don't know what we are. I don't even know if I care enough to ask the question."

"That's probably the right answer."

Carl lets that sit a moment, allowing a silence to settle in. The sounds of night creep back, their familiar swell and ebb filling a void that moment creates and fosters. All this broken by the reappearance of talk as Carl shifts tacks, first with face, slackened skin and jaw agape, then with words, friendly, almost concerned.

"Are you happy?"

"What's that matter?"

"Doesn't. I just want to know your answer."

Hat doesn't respond.

"Nobody answers honestly. Almost nobody. Hardly anybody. You've got people who wish they were happy, those people don't answer. People who don't want to think about it so they dodge the question. Broken people hold onto that shit, ponder it like they do any question, like it has some greater meaning. Like anything does. You know what happy people do? They say yes."

Carl sits a minute, waiting for Hat to weigh in, but he does not. Animals move in the night, the world itself writhing under the weight of the moment. Birds fly in aimless circuits, as if nature itself has lost its way.

Carl speaks again.

"Sometimes you encounter something. You come up against this thing and it's just too big to incorporate into your world. You get left standing on the outside of this alien concept and you either abandon yourself to it or you harden yourself and run the thing down. You're looking for a why. For why we do this, or why it matters. Why doesn't come into it. Why is a non-factor. Maybe it's not good against evil, but it's something."

"What we do, it's not like this in stories," says Hat. "In books."

"That's not what brought you here. That doesn't matter to you."

"Doesn't it?"

"What do you think it should be?" asks Carl, a sudden snarl of words that belies the otherwise cavalier demeanor. "Hoodoo and shit? Draw some lines around? That doesn't work. If that shit works, I haven't seen it. Everything dies if you put enough holes through it. These things aren't fairytale monsters. You can't wish them away. They're like anybody. The regulars follow orders, they play it like a chess game. They move, we move, like that. And the other ones. Free spirits. Independent messes that rain down upon the earth like a biblical plague."

The light in Carl, the harsh malevolence that for only moments shown not just in features but in every pore, every breath, this thing subsides, leaving behind only wistful rumination.

"This world is an innocent. Spared of the nightmare that we know. We are the caretakers of thoughts. The way they were before the world got to them. Before they turned dark."

The weight of words slips by. Hat reaches for the unturned crevices within the syllables but stops short of asking to hear them spoken plainly, afraid letting them back into the world might allow them to lose all meaning. He speaks up.

"A man stopped me. He stopped by me. I thought he wanted something but he only stood there, not looking at me. Facing me but I don't know. I wasn't what he was seeing. He asked me about life. I don't think I gave him the right answer."

Carl listens, absorbing the words but no longer an active participant, only letting their pregnant tale wash over him in a meaningful tide. He nods at times or just looks out at what lies in front. He speaks no further, and Hat fails to notice the lack of interchange, only carries on with what he has to say. The story goes on as long as it should, and soon there is a fire in the east that is a new day's start.

———

A man sits on a stool along the sidewalk. A vendor. A card table is stacked with newspapers, magazines, trash that will be soon forgotten. The man nods an oddly shaped head at people as they pass, but he does not look up with his odd, melted face, only goes on letting his eyes wander over the words in a battered paperback. A woman stops and flips through a magazine but she does not buy. She smiles at the man but he doesn't see and soon she is gone.

Hat's walk is aimless, its destination unknown. He stops at the table not to buy a paper but only because he recognizes the man. He says hello and the man nods without looking up.

The papers are stacked high, few sold this early in the day. Hat doesn't know he's going to buy one until he does. He slips cash under the lip of a magazine, tapping it once, twice, drawing just enough notice. He flips through the paper, not looking for anything, this venture as aimless as the last. Sales, scandals, pablum. He pauses briefly on the story of an unidentified man found dead, shot, this pale and broken man belonging to no one. Hat reads through the story but there isn't much there. Done, he folds the paper under arm and moves on.

"Your change," says the vendor without looking up.

"It's alright," says Hat over his shoulder, not slowing.

The vendor reads on. He licks a finger and turns a page and the story continues unbroken.

"This is the best part," he says, but there is no one around.

GANG OF 21

Part 1 - The Beast

Carl is off his meds.

Biting white fluorescents watch over his awkward progress through aisles lined by rows of candies whose shining labels flaunt baffling names and loud color schemes. He squints under that light's gaze as a wide, amiable grin cuts a swath through his face where a slack mouth should be. A fist-sized bell hangs above the door but no chime comes as patrons enter or leave. The door is propped open with a warm case of cheap beer. It's not quite morning.

A plastic clock on the counter pounds away the seconds as the needle hand wanders in circles. A radio sits next to it but plays only static. The man behind the counter is Dave something. He has more name but no one ever asks. The nametag he wears on his baby blue smock spells out the name Paco in lumps of black letters. It was picked at random. Anything less generic than Dave. He wears sunglasses so no one can see his eyes. He thinks of himself as tough but misunderstood. The kind of guy who might lead cops on a two hour car chase but will still wave at oncoming traffic the whole way. Not aggressive back and forth waves. Passive ones, fingers all together, palm still on the wheel. Casual. Wide, flat teeth gnaw on a stick of candy made from anything but sugar.

This is Dave. The baffling quote in tomorrow's paper attributed to a witness at the scene will be straight from his slack mouth.

The coolers sweat. Carl squints at labels on water but they all say the same thing in different fonts. A giant beast of a man with acres of hairless head gapes at one cooler after another. Six feet easy. Six and a half. Maybe more. Carl catches sight of his hovering. The giant smiles like he knows a secret. A smell surrounds him like a halo. Thick, cloying. Something harsh but sweet, like flowers in a closet. He waits with unwavering patience while Carl stands with the cooler door open and stares blankly at the dozens of brands of bottled water. He grabs one at random and steps back. The giant grabs the door's handle the breadth of a moment before it can close and wraps huge meaty fingers around a foreign bottle of bland carbonated water. Fascist.

Dave hasn't moved, maybe hasn't breathed. He could be in a coma. A taxidermied clerk. Carl sets down the water, lays at its side a crumpled note, flattening out the page with one smooth palm.

"Need a pick up."

Dave leans forward to read the details of what may once have been a prescription. A doctor's name screams across a line at the bottom in a maniac scrawl.

"Pharmacy doesn't open for a couple hours."

He gives an audible lick of whatever half-assed confection he's wasting his time on as Carl looks past him at the library of pills beyond. A sigh and a shrug change nothing.

"Just the water, then."

Change spreads on the counter. Carl digs out pennies first. Dave watches, or at least his glasses do. Three counts and never the same number. Heavy footfalls halt behind but there is no other sound. Dave takes up counting, going through the coins already counted as Carl pushes more across the counter just to fuck with him. Forty-nine, fifty, fifty-one. He counts again and Carl wipes hands on his shirt.

New footfalls. Nimble but not light.

"Do you have a pen?"

Dave glances up. His mouth goes on silently tasting numbers. Seventy-two, seventy-three, seventy-four. Carl looks over his shoulder. The giant bald beast stares at the rows of cigarettes behind the counter, line after line of delicious sin standing at parade rest. The man who spoke is diminutive in the shadow of that giant, the smaller man patting pockets and looking around as if a pen might be found on the floor, was there all along. His glasses are huge and crooked, his hair slicked but beginning to stand out in places, a wild glee displayed on pasty features. His suit is too big, bulging in places, hanging limp from his wiry frame. A lit cigarette dangles from a pouty lip. A maniac Buddy Holly breathing smoke and hovering in a baggy, moth-eaten suit. This newcomer winks at Carl and asks his question again to no one in particular.

"Can I get a pen?"

Dave counts with one hand and passes over a black ink pen with the other. A buck ten. A buck eleven. A buck twelve. The pen is nice, not cheap. Ballpoint with someone's initials stamped in the side. Maybe someone loved this pen.

A lithe hand shoves the pen into an inner pocket of the oversized, comical suit. The hand moves fast, comes back with a snub thirty-eight held in a professional grip. An ugly little thing, chips in the finish where someone hit it against something hard in a struggle or when tossing it from a moving vehicle once or many times.

"Thanks."

The man in the oversized suit puts the squat gun to that giant hairless skull. A look of realization appears and swells in the eyes of the beast. Realization and something else. A hate, deep and eternal. This well of emotion is unalterably erased in an explosion of violence as the thirty-eight goes off.

His voice jumps up and down as he talks, the man in the loose suit. His cigarette falls out of his mouth and falls to the floor, leaving a trail of gray soot as it rolls down his suit and comes to rest in against the giant sprawled leg of the body. Smoke leaks from the lip of the gun as he makes his case.

"It's okay. He was an angel."

Silence from the others. He elaborates.

"In a bad way."

The fickle passage of time goes on. Dave leans over the counter and looks at the corpse. Gore drips from the ads that hang above the counter.

"Shit."

Dave goes back to his near comatose stance. He's said his piece.

The man in the suit takes a backward step toward the door, then another.

"Don't call the cops."

He takes another step. Carl looks at the corpse. The heavy aroma of flowers blooms in the room. The face is a ruin. Blood pools like a gruesome pond. The body starts to move. Carl puts up a hand to contain his gasp. It gets out anyway.

"Jesus fuck!"

The gun barks again. The corpse is once more a corpse.

"Sometimes they're obstinate."

The man takes another step back.

Carl puts up a hand. Hailing a cab.

"Can I come?"

The man's eyes narrow. Suspicious. The thirty-eight comes up, not quite pointing at Carl and not quite not.

"Are you some kind of crazy?"

Carl shrugs.

"Do you have a car?"

Carl beams.

"Sort of."

The gun lowers to the man's side, hangs in a loose right hand. The left digs in one pocket after another until it comes up with the pen. This goes into clenched teeth as he digs again, this time finding a five dollar bill. He steps forward once more, a ginger step over the body to get to the counter. The left hand sets the bill on top of the piles of change and scribbles words across Lincoln's unimpeachable face. Dave has lost count.

Fast scrawl of pen on paper ends in a flourish. He dots an imagined letter somewhere in the heart of the message left behind and looks around as he recaps the pen with one hand.

"Gross."

His exit is cavalier as he moves through the aisles. The way he snags a bag of candied peanuts, it's like he's been casually stealing all his life. He doesn't look back as he rounds the corner and enters the world. Carl is only a step behind.

Half a dozen seconds pass before Dave begins to fumble unsteady hands over a telephone handset. He works the buttons with the awkwardness of an adolescent discovering the unique trap that is a bra latch for the first time. Hands freeze as eyes find the words plastered over the face of a dead president.

Sorry for the mess. Jesus saves.

———

The cab is probably stolen. Carl mutters something about having a license but doesn't explain what kind. Driver's license, cabbie's license. He keeps both somewhere in his world. Both are long expired.

"I'm Gus, in case it comes up."

The floppy suit hangs loose as he sinks deep into the worn fabric of the seat. He gestures a lazy hand this way or that when he wants Carl to turn. Most of his time is taken up chewing peanuts layered with a pink candy coating and talking through the mush in his gaping mouth.

"You probably have a lot of questions."

Hand points left. Carl shrugs as he takes the turn.

"Not really."

Gus chews and grins and pretends he doesn't hear.

"It's usually demons. That's what we're about. Killing demons."

His face scrunches up in an expression so earnest it must have taken years of practice to master. A child's impression of sincerity.

"It's the Lord's work."

The relaxed chewing returns on cue. A switch flipped.

"Angels are kind of a curiosity. We don't get many because they're, you know, usually good. And we've got three!"

A slender hand flashes out to fidget with the radio dial. He goes on chewing and never stays on any station for more than a few seconds. They pass a man on the sidewalk reading a wrinkled newspaper. His hair stands in hard tufts sculpted with gel or soap. Hand points left. Car follows hand.

"Angels, I mean. Three angels."

He stops the dial on a droning ad for a lawyer who has fiery words about an imagined villain who needs to be sued.

"Do you know the difference between a fallen angel and a demon?"

Carl drives on. He says nothing. Gus chews and talks and an indifferent hand points left.

"Don't worry about it. Not your problem. Not even my problem. It's some middleman's problem, and those guys couldn't give fuck one about our concerns. They'll cough in an envelope and send it to God, not bother explaining the question. Like He already knows. Sees you when you're sleeping, knows when you're awake, that old gag. It's a brave new world. What were you saying?"

Carl says nothing. They take another left.

"Anyway, three angels."

The bag is empty, the peanuts gone. They pass a man reading a wrinkled paper. He runs a hand through spiked hair, knocking loose strands of coarse black. A line of utility poles march off through every street passed. A watermark of civilization. This is the only recognizable landmark. The buildings are all withered, crumbling tenements from decades long dead. The streets are all cracked macadam, pockmarked lanes winding off to unknown futures, their hopes all scarred and ruined. Even the sky is a stranger in this place.

"Not nice ones. We've been calling them the Gang of Twenty-One. As a, like a, a tongue in cheek thing. The Three Sevens. Gang of Twenty-One. For Heaven. You get me."

Gus looks out the window as they pass a man with spiked hair reading a wrinkled paper. His shoulders square in lingering brood.

"It's a cute name, right?"

Carl shrugs and turns left.

Familiar power lines drape down from above, cinched to the world but to nothing else like the loose strings of a marionette untethered to the skillful hand of a knowing puppeteer. Atop pole after pole sit carrion birds, fat black lumps with feathers like oil and shrewd eyes that absorb the world below. Somewhere nearby, something is dead.

1998

Part 2 - The Corruptor

The doctor looks like the good-humored TV dad from a '50s sit-com no one ever watched. His name is Jacks. He scrawls thoughts on a scrip pad while offering the occasional noncommittal nod. Notes for a children's book about a lemur eking out a living as a therapist or sometimes a detective. Margins are dotted with doodles of lunatic monkeys riding crudely drawn elephants or monster syringes. Colorless attempts at imagination wind their way through lines on a page where elaborately named drugs should be written in a saner hand.

Dr. Jacks no longer listens to Carl. Not really.

They meet once a week. Sometimes twice. The office is a cramped, unhappy place for patients on a budget. A closet in a former life. Carl goes on and on, smiling and offering up detailed accounts of personal, intimate encounters with fabled creatures straight out of arcane biblical texts and half understood foreign folk tales. He says it all in a pragmatic, isn't-it-just-so-funny kind of tone that expects an accepting audience of this listener and finds one nodding enough to be just that.

He takes up the hour, exorcises the sins of the week in a ritual cleanse, finishes with a hazy afterthought about needing to get to work. The doctor sits in a pocket of silence, finishing a doodle and realizing the talking has found its end. He says something pleasant, friendly, appeasing, and scribbles a quick prescription for something Carl won't bother picking up.

———

Highway traffic. The ride from the airport to downtown is sluggish but not stalled. Carl taps a bored thumb on the wheel of a black foreign monster belonging to someone higher up than he. His passengers are new, a couple of rogues he's never before seen around. Strangers.

The bodyguard sits up front. His face is pounded from hard clay into a more or less human shape, a face frozen in the perpetual grimace of a man who only moments before took a punch to the gut, that gut-punch grimace never fading, only staring out the window with shrewd, calculating eyes.

The man in back turns page after page of a dog-eared self help paperback, sporadically taking a moment to lick a stark white finger of the latex gloves that cling to his hands before turning a page and continuing on his way to personal enlightenment. A thin crop of hair combed back from a fierce widows peak stands out in an angry V atop an unwrinkled head. Tinted windows leave the backseat passenger in premature night, a weak blue fighting its way through that tinting, but the reading carries on undaunted.

The job is a snap. It always is. Pick up lunatics and take them to lunatic places so they can do their lunatic things. Piousness shouldn't be this easy. Self-flagellation is for suckers.

Carl bobs his head to no song at all. The radio is silent, all the preset stations set to the moody talk radio another driver prefers to ingest, bent over the wheel, all white-knuckles and brimstone. Carl doesn't realize his slight seat dancing is occurring until he spots the guard's square mug pouting his way, those shrewd eyes glistening somewhere inside that mound of flesh. He looks to the mirror to find pinprick pupils returning his gaze from the backseat as the paperback lowers an inch or two.

"You're new."

Carl returns his eyes to the road, then back to the mirror.

"Not really."

The pop psych paperback falls from view, finds itself poised open page down on a knee. A gloved hand runs over the shellacked V of hair. Not a single strand is moved.

"Tell me about corruption."

Traffic begins to pick up speed. Carl's attention tries to stay on the millions of angry motorists splayed out in every direction as he tries to answer as best he can.

"What?"

"Corruption. What is it?"

Carl isn't nervous. A normal man would be nervous, he knows a normal man would be unnerved by the wild way the backseat man's eyes dance in his head, but Carl only shrugs. The man leans forward, those gloved hands latching onto the headrests of the front seats as he speaks in a precise accent.

"Corruption is a cancer. Lies poison men just as cancer rots a bowel. Sickness spreads in institutions from one man to a thousand and soon the whole system is a ruin, a shell hollowed out, its insides brought low by that single thread of sickness allowed to grow. Corruption is men. Lies. Cancer. Sin. We are all sinners. We are corruption."

Carl puts his foot on the gas as a blue haired hag honks the intense horn in her diminutive German bubble of a car. Carl gives her the finger and moves on down the road. He smiles over his shoulder as he talks to the backseat man.

"Yeah, I guess I am new. But I'm thinking about staying."

———

They call him Boston Jack. Not to Carl. To Carl they say nothing. Hard men with unfriendly faces enter the diner portion of an eatery that's lost its way. One part bar, one part restaurant, in its youth a weekend hotspot for the swells, the decadent remains of its existence being lived out as a weekday dive for the young and poor. The afternoon has yet to give up the ghost and the men have the place more or less to themselves. They gather around a corner booth, all hushed tones and expectation. Jack and his guard, Gus and a fat man in a Hawaiian shirt, a tired man who sits apart from the others and quietly drinks deep gulps of some archaic concoction, a vile broth leaving stains on the rim of his glass like an oil spill. And another man, a slender man in a modest suit, the kind of thing worn for work, a blue collar soul with a white collar tailor. This one, this slim face carved from soap with his suit of wool armor, this is the centerpiece. This is who they've come to see.

No one bothers telling Carl who this man is. To Carl they say nothing.

The bar is across a spacious lounge from the farce these men play out. Carl gravitates, not to the drink but to the bargirl sipping a shot of something clear and leaning over the bar, one hand holding her chin. Bored.

He points a finger at nothing in particular several feet above her head and speaks.

"That."

The petite thing reaches up to aim a finger at the line of bottles. A pile of dark curls fall around a pale face. A hint of soft belly peaks out from under the shirt, not milk white but painted, ink stained with personality, a slow reveal until appears a tattooed hockey mask and two crossed sticks. Faux Jolly Roger.

Her hand slides along the line, a slow seduction of boozes until, still with eyes on that belly fresco, Carl speaks up with casual indifference.

"Yeah."

He isn't looking at what she pulls down and begins to pour, only takes it and sips, sips again, and down. He nods thanks but she's already returned to her perch on the bar, that hand back up, soft curve of chin nestled in its jaded grasp.

The antics in the corner booth continue. Carl wants none of it.

The front door has no chime, and no one turns as he exits. An ancient man with a flat frog mouth sits on a sidewalk bench watching cars race by at excessive speeds.

"Bunch of dogs is all."

Carl laughs at the sandpaper gruff voice that comes from that frog mouth, only stopping as he realizes that voice, those words, they are not a put on. Fingers stained bruise yellow by a lifelong affair with nicotine tap out a weak pulse on the knee of worn corduroys. A bulbous cartoon thumb points over a shoulder so the old man can make good and sure it's clear which dogs he's referring to. An opaque layer of disregard that cakes the window blocks the finer points of detail that make the inside of the restaurant a vivid picture show, but the indistinct splotches shaped like men are clear enough. Carl rubs a sleeve over the grime and the picture comes into focus. The talk continues. The man in the middle, the blue collar centerpiece in the modest suit runs his mouth with little animation, the occasional gesture of a worn hand. Talking as they listen.

Out front, the old man's fingers tap to the beat of some forgotten song.

"Them dogs like to hear all that barking. Don't change a thing."

The man in the Hawaiian shirt sneezes into one meaty hand. Heads turn, one after another, each man looking at the hand wavering in the air as another sneeze comes. The centerpiece goes on speaking, an angel happy to share all he knows and all he is with the men who would gather to hear.

Gus begins to cough.

"Them dogs lie," says the old man.

The cough spreads fast. The man with the oily drink watches through watery eyes as the glass falls from his hand and shatters on the floor. Still the angel in the modest suit prattles on, his story not yet finished.

"Don't ever trust no angel."

The bodyguard with the clay face waits. The man with the fierce widow's peak, Boston Jack holds up a hand as his eyes squint and his face turns the sickly pink of dying fruit. Only when that prohibiting hand drops does the bodyguard draw his weapon and execute the talking angel where he sits.

"They lie just like anybody."

The coughs sputter and stall. The sickness slowly fades.

1999

Part 3 - The Possessor

There are no locks here but still no one leaves.

The room is expansive and cramped at the same time. Long and wide but short, diminutive, demoralizing. The tables are rounded. Everywhere things are rimmed with soft rubber. A bubble wrap world, completely safe. No danger lurks around the corner because there are no corners here. Patients are watched by an omniscient stranger who hides behind the lens of one camera or all of them. Watches so no one gets creative and opens a vein with the edge of a chair or a sharpened straw from a smuggled juice box.

Carl makes his move but he is terrible at chess. Whites so he goes first. It doesn't matter. His pieces are all over the place. Blacks sit still, lined up in their places, waiting for a move to make. A Maginot Line sitting there in judgment, not realizing the rules of the game have changed completely.

Arthur watches from across the room in a round white chair for as long as he can take. Carl doesn't look up but feels eyes scratching at the skin of his hands as he moves each piece. Arthur isn't Arthur's real name and who knows what it is. He calls himself The Bull but denies the name was his idea. He grins like a fiend and his head is flanked by his shoulders. He deserves to be here.

"What are you doing, crazy?"

Arthur says crazy like he's winning a contest. Heaving a pile of letters across the room. He never says who or what he's so angry at and his counselor is McReady so it will probably never be clear.

Carl eyeballs the door before he answers. Not locked. This one or any of them. The front door is wide open but he sits still.

"Losing."

Arthur gets up and moves over to the table. He reaches for a black piece but doesn't touch. Testing. He looks at the soft round chair pushed out from the round table but doesn't sit down. Looks at Carl, looks at the chair. He look at the pieces.

"You gonna be around later, crazy?"

Carl nods and does not look up. Maybe he laughs.

"What will you be doing then?"

He nods minutely at the pushed out chair.

"Probably playing chess with my party."

Arthur "The Bull" Marx snorts and wraps his long coat around his middle.

"Be careful, crazy. Alliteration is the artwork of the devil."

"No it's not."

No it's not.

———

Group meets at 2 o'clock. Session is usually led by Docs Thompson or Avery. Both are off at some conference they won't talk about. Dissecting live subjects into bite size snacks. Testing pills on unsuspecting tourists. Jacks is running things today. McReady is sitting in. Observing. These names, bullshit. Whitebread obfuscation. They bark amongst themselves in bitter German grunts when they think no one is listening.

Katie and Roman sit next to each other talking about daytime talk shows. Others wander in when they're good and ready. Most of these schlubs have been here for years but outside of group no one ever hears them speak. Arthur sits across from Carl. If someone tries to sit in the seat next to him he shoos them away. The oblong runny sacks he calls eyes look Carl's way each time he does it. Saving a seat for Carl's friends, he calls it. Condescending fuck.

"How are we today, class?"

Reginald Jacks doesn't like to refer to them as patients. No one is insane anymore. People aren't crazy. Students of a level mind, he says. Emotional bricklayer that he is, most of the inmates buy into it. Carl eyes the door and ignores the shouts of SCHNELL! SCHNELL! drifting in from some far off hallway.

"I'm still having those dreams."

Katie doesn't have any dreams. Her overpaid posh parents don't know how to raise her so they send her here. It's cheaper than private prep school and in modern society looks just as good on a resume.

One of the wrinkled foreigners who come to group but never speak shits himself and wanders away from the circle of rounded chairs. Arthur hitches up his pants like he's going to say something wise but doesn't. Roman fills the void.

"What time is it?"

Katie scratches at her arms and tries not to let her words come out in a snarl.

"It's a quarter after two, Roman. Group meets at two. We've been sitting here a few minutes. What the fuck is wrong with you?"

Roman is crazy. Roman eats trinkets and money and small electronic gadgets so others can't take them away from him. Roman forgets his meds and wanders around ranting or he takes other people's and sits in his own drool and filth for days at a time. Roman is a fucking mess.

"Roman is studying to flatten his world. He's been working hard for some time and has made great leaps toward this end. What about you, Carl? What do you have to share today?"

Dr. Jacks holds that academic facade up like a riot shield but Carl sees the gleam of madness hiding just behind. Sometimes he wonders if the doctor is a patient wearing the face of one of his former counselors like a calm, nurturing, fleshy mask.

"I think things are changing."

The doctor's eyebrows do a nosedive but Carl does not believe their sincerity for an instant.

"How is that?"

"I haven't been seeing them lately."

Arthur almost turns over his chair in his rush to jump in.

"He's lying! He told me to save this seat for one of them! Don't buy that bullshit he's peddling!"

They double Carl's dosage for the next two nights.

———

The television is muted and several minutes go by before he realizes the voice speaking is his own. He doesn't know what he's saying and it doesn't matter. He stops talking and the voice goes on a moment longer. He reaches up to wipe his mouth but his arm is echo slow, his mind outrunning it by seconds.

"You can leave any time, Carl. They only tell you you can't to test you."

The stranger sitting next to Carl in a soft round chair doesn't look as he speaks. His eyes stay forward, aimless, wandering around the room tasting its many subtle flavors. Those eyes are wrong, the pupils too large and the whites not white, more yellow with wild pools of red blood where something is going or has gone horribly wrong. His pajamas are light fabric, dirty and dark in color, held together by will. He wears no shoes and his feet are marked by stains of life. His face is milk white, blue veins crawling through like a roadmap to some arcane hell. A wild shock of black hair stands atop that pale skull. A faint pleasant smell surrounds, a suggestion of flowers. He is not a patient and he is not a doctor.

When Carl closes his eyes he forgets the stranger's face completely.

Katie drinks a green liquid from a clear cup and flirts with a doctor but his back is to Carl and he doesn't know which one. Dr. McReady looms in a corner telling lies to a patient named Michaels or Nichols. People move through the dayroom but no one sees Carl's visitor and they do not look his way.

Carl's eyes move and his face follows and he looks at his visitor, this stranger, as that pale skull with its wrong eyes takes in the measure of the room. His legs are crossed at the knee and hands rest in lap, folded and inert. The posture should seem effeminate but lacks the connotation utterly. His words wander through Carl's head a time or two but their substance is ethereal and before long they aren't there at all. His mind reaches for them again to run his fingers over the texture of their meaning but they connect with only air and he is left empty. A window set into the wall is double paned with wire mesh tucked between. The sky on the other side of those layers of glass and resistance reddens and curdles and thick black clouds crawl in to take up residence in the peace of the world. His lips are numb and the words that slip past them are slow to take form.

"How odd. I thought it was still day out."

————

The voice on the radio talks mostly about a violin. An old one made from trees cut down centuries ago. It is worth a fortune to anyone needing an old violin. The voice is thick with rasp, the kind of throaty husk that comes from drinking and smoking all night. There is a hint of slur in the voice, maybe accent, maybe not. The voice should be the incessant wale of a repetitive buzz but no matter how many times Carl changes the clock radio at his bedside to an alarm it always goes off as an opinionated man with something to sell the next morning.

The radio is on the list of prohibited items.

The sheets are on the floor and Katie wraps a blanket around herself before leaving. Only now does Carl wonder what she was wearing when she came in. The only sound is the slap of her bare feet moving down the hall. A moment later the sound is played backward and a secret message hides within. Her face peeks around the corner, short dark locks curve around the delicate cream skin of a young face.

"If it makes you feel any better, I don't think you're crazy."

She disappears once more and the sound of her feet follows along. Carl lies there for minutes wondering just what she means.

————

Dr. Avery is woefully unqualified to treat or diagnose. He drinks in the bathroom before each meeting. Private session should go on upstairs in one of the offices but it never does. They come to patients. Sometimes in the dayroom, that waving field of off-white tile with its air of protection from all things real, more often in personal suites, away from prying eyes and the safety of that God living in his surveillance cam heaven.

"I never said I didn't believe you."

His tone is buttered in a fattening layer of arrogance. He is smarter than Carl and Carl is too stupid to notice. Avery bounces his foot as it hangs over his other knee like a bored kid in church.

"I don't care if you believe me or not. It doesn't change anything."

He writes something in his notebook as it rests on his leg, bounces along with the foot. The handwriting must be awful.

"Tell me more about these vampires."

Carl licks his upper lip and tries not to roll his eyes.

"Who said vampire? I never said vampire."

Dr. Avery's head tilts down to look at his notes. The eyes come back up but the head stays down. Carl is the fool, so silly, so naive. Avery is the parent, forgiving, understanding.

"It says right here, They come when I'm off my medication. Who are these vampires, Carl?"

His quotes are fictions of his own madness. The apparitions come when Carl is off or they come when he's on. They come whenever they want and he knows these things are real.

"They aren't vampires. They're not all men, but they aren't vampires."

Avery's eyes drop for a moment.

"Do they tell you to do things?"

They tell Carl to leave this place. They tell him these men are fools and liars. Sinners and the damned. They tell him he should be out doing God's work. They tell him it's his job.

"Yeah, they tell me to sue. You think I can't smell the gin on your breath?"

Avery makes another notation, longer this time. Long breaths widen his nostrils. He flips a page or two back in the notebook and lets a pause thicken in the room.

"What about Gus, Carl?"

He stares at Avery until the doctor looks up. He continues to stare until he looks down again.

"I think we've made good progress today."

———

A stack of paper and a ballpoint pen sit before Carl. A letter waits unwritten. He picks up the pen and puts it back down. He picks it up again and holds it. The casing is cheap plastic. Lines shape its form into a small octagonal tube instead of the smooth circle he hopes for. There is something awkward and unnecessary in this. The ink runs out on the page as he sits staring.

The point of the pen is tiny and fierce, a crude weapon created to capture the raging attacks of man's mind on paper for all to see. The table is round and edgeless, a flat earth for men to sail off of. The pen is not on the prohibited items list. All these little contradictions.

———

The dayroom stinks of burned coffee. Carl pushes pieces around the board but his heart isn't in it. He's blacks. Whites don't bother to go. The chair across from him is empty but the room is full of crazy people and they don't know that.

"Turn that up!" says Roman with a crack of misplaced adrenaline. Carl wants to turn to see what they see on the television but his heart isn't in it. He picks up his king and holds it in his palm.

"Hey Carl, you're on TV," says Katie. He looks at her and not the screen as he responds.

"That's not me."

Guilt or gloom or some mix of both twist in his gut as she holds his gaze a moment longer, a look of dawning sadness spreading on her features. Arthur stands over him with a notebook in hand and Carl breaks the grip of her eyes. The notebook is set down on the chessboard. Avery's notes. The Bull doesn't say how he got them. Scribbled, bounced script wandering the page. Sarcastic despair. Doodles and insults circle a single bleak word that tightens the grip on doom. There is no redemption here.

Hopeless.

———

Dr. Jacks gives awkward licks at the phone during long pauses. Carl looks away and hopes the doctor hasn't seen that he's been found out. His tone when he does speak is too even, inhuman, narcotized. He talks about the mundane and nods into the phone and hangs up. Moments roll out, thick with tension and waiting to break. And then they do.

"What's this I'm hearing about you and Katie?"

"I'm an inmate. You can't evict me."

"You're a patient, not an inmate."

"So I can go then?"

"Your behavior is beginning to be a problem."

"Maybe somebody should lock me up."

"We have rules for a reason."

"What if I'm not crazy?"

Dr. Jacks clears his throat and clears it again to make a point. His response almost seems redundant.

"That avenue hardly seems worth pursuing."

———

Group is late. Patients are excused for something upstairs. A birthday, maybe. Katie sits in a round blue chair, her feet tucked underneath her as she writes lies in a journal. Arthur grins like a fool and taps a foot in anticipation. Dr. Thompson leans back in his chair with his arms crossed, that cold visage unmoved by the rise and fall of a thousand empires. Carl waits.

No one else has come.

Thompson doesn't ask a question, doesn't suggest someone go first, merely nods in Carl's direction.

"I want to talk about something different today."

Katie looks up from her scribbling.

"I've been lying. None of the things I've said are true. The man shot in the pharmacy? He was no angel. That giant beast of a man was just a man. And Gus. They called him Fun Gus sometimes. Did I tell you that? He wasn't real. I made him up."

Inexplicable tears begin to roll down Katie's soft cheeks, leaving a streak of black eye shadow. Arthur begins to rub at his face, his eyes. His grin grows wider.

"And then there was the one who spread disease. The angel who lied, told untruths to the others, infecting them first with those lies and then with another kind of sickness. An angel who could corrupt bodies and minds. He wasn't real. A trick of the mind."

The journal falls to the floor as Katie mumbles a halfhearted excuse and hurries out of the room. Dr. Thompson sits as stone, his chest barely rising and falling. Some of Arthur's color has begun to drain but his grin pulls at the edges of his face as his amusement redoubles.

"None of it happened. None of it's real. The whole story. The Gang of Twenty-One. It was a flight of fancy. That third angel, they never found him. They never found him because he didn't exist in the first place."

Arthur laughs. Abrupt, wild guffaws that should choke off his air but don't, only roll out stronger and meaner for what seems like minutes. His eyes fill with blood and his lips blacken as the fight to breathe through that maddening laughter finds more and more it's easier to just give in. Hard blue veins stick out of the strained skin of that face and still the laughter barks its way into the world.

All at once it ceases, cut off.

"You're such a fucking liar."

It's Arthur's mouth speaking, but the voice is that of a stranger.

THE BOOK OF SAMUEL

1. Now

Nobody smokes anymore. Distracted faces march by in lockstep, an endless stream of humanity playing out forever in every direction. Fingers tap on phones or heads bob to some private song, faces staring hard into holes behind their own eyes, wanderers downing vitamin water or lips moving in private conversation with entities present or imagined, and on and on it goes, this advancing procession of non-smokers with no beginning or end.

A man lounges, back pressed to old brick, the heat of sun on street and the flow of multitudes washing over him in waves. An unlit cigarette dangles from his lip. He has no lighter, or if he does he does not use it. He stands and he watches, mouth slack, looking but not seeing as the world passes by.

He steps into the stream.

He moves, carried along by that flow of bodies. Storefronts pass, a sandwich shop, a book store, until he finds himself standing beneath an unlit sign's single welcoming word. BAR.

Mildewed air escapes in a chilled sigh as he pulls open the door and steps into darkness. The floor slopes downward for the first few feet, drawing entrants in with its subtle, inevitable descent. Heads turn at the intrusion of light. Not many, not at this hour; an elderly man with a po-boy and a whiskey, a few innocent twenty-somethings manhandling imported beers over sparse bouts of trite talk.

A pale waif with a head of dark curls mans the bar. She nods at the man.

"Sam," she says.

He unfolds a twenty pulled from some inner pocket, places it on the carved bar surface. She pours two fingers of dark liquid into a glass. He drinks it down and she pours another. Sweat beads on glass skin, a clear pool spreading at the base with the fall of each drop.

Hours pass in the swirl and thrum of a thousand ephemeral faces. They order drinks and they spin and erupt with mad talk of all the lives they will live or have lived, all manner of thought and of feeling on full display in some corner or other as bodies pile in and night takes hold.

"Are you gonna smoke that?"

A face in the maelstrom. She's drunk, this face, this stranger. She points at the unlit cigarette Samuel holds loose between two fingers. Her lip curls in earnest, unchecked contempt. He shrugs. He's been bathed in her drunken, self-important rambling for minutes. The bartender slides by, smirking at the scene, on her way to pour thin rums or fetch green bottles of some chilled something for the wanting multitude.

She talks, the stranger does, and he doesn't listen but she doesn't notice and soon she has drifted away as night becomes something else, some late hour careening toward inescapable morning.

Samuel eyes the passage of a figure reflected in the mirror behind the bar. This newcomer moves with assured gait through the pressing crowd. Samuel stands, his tepid drink still on the bar with a cigarette left unsmoked.

The bathroom stinks of lemon and vomit and something else, something worse. The newcomer stands by a sink run through with cracks. Water drips from tap. The man speaks into a phone in a language all edges and menace. Something old, the tongue of a people dead and lost. He keeps his back turned.

The bathroom's single stall cants to one side, bolts bent or gone, its connection to the wall tenuous, fragile. Stickers and flyers for bands already defunct paper every surface, layered in places, the pages in front obscuring the ghosts of dead dreams that hide underneath. Samuel pisses and flushes and the man goes on talking or shouting, now moving, agitated, loafers tapping on hard floor as he paces the few feet of space. His face remains turned away. Samuel runs water, wets hands. There is no soap.

An odor comes off the man in waves, a stink of corruption from within. Something sweet with sickness. The man curses in English and ends the call. He stares at the phone, waiting for something to come that never does. He leaves. Water is left forgotten and pouring at a casual trickle as Samuel follows.

Through the bar and out. Hot night air hits flesh with force, pulls breath from lungs. The BAR sign now hums with life. A car passes, a song playing on a radio, notes slipping through the open window of a fleeting moment, now there, receding, now gone. A melody familiar but out of reach. The man watches the car's taillights disappear in the distance as he moves with that same confident step along an empty street for blocks.

The building he enters is a dull crate filled with homes and lives, a tenement aged and withering among miles of the same. He climbs a flight of stairs. A woman sleeps on a couch on the landing. He climbs a second flight and enters an apartment.

Samuel follows. The woman on the landing stirs as he passes but if she wakes he has already gone. He stops outside the door to the man's apartment. One hand on the doorknob. He takes the gun from his coat. He turns the knob and pushes open the door.

That inhuman reek is thick here, overwhelming in the den of the thing that looks like a man. Skin hangs loose. Eyes swollen and jaundiced. It holds papers, mail. These things it sets down. It steps back, pushes closed a cracked door and obscures whatever is hidden on the other side. It speaks flat words, tone casual, an accent dense and impossible to place.

"Who are you?"

"I'm Sam."

"Why are you wearing a coat?"

A handful of seconds slip off the clock. World sounds play, the movement and rattle of life. Televisions talk or laugh, footfalls thump in rooms above. Samuel raises the weapon and shoots once. A spray of blood and mess. The thing drops, stone dead. Samuel's arm lowers to his side, weapon dangling, no longer relevant. The sounds of the world persist in every direction, unchanged and uninterested in the moment's drama. Samuel stands that way, a statue in the midst of a moving, shifting universe, still looking at the unmoving thing on the floor long after the need to do so has passed.

—————

Cool morning breeze drifts in through a back door propped open. The bartender watches television light flicker. Infomercial, a wild man discussing pillows. Slate gray studio. He gestures and moves and he talks about allergies. He tells a joke. An audience laughs.

Tables are littered with the chaos of last night; bottles and glasses, wads of napkin, a few tossed dollars, ones or fives. A man sits at the end of the bar, a paperback veiling the cherubic detail of a round baby face. Band t-shirt, something from a long ago tour, lettering flaked and blacks faded gray. Samuel sits slumped in a high-backed stool midway across the bar, a half empty bottle near at hand. A glass is drained and waiting.

There is a flood of street sound as the front door opens. The static rustle of countless feet on pavement, tires on street, engine hum and talk and wind. The morning cool begins its inexorable ebb. A man moves down the ramp. Loose jeans and ball cap. He stops and he sits beside the man with the book. An envelope smacks bar top surface two times, three times.

"Sam, hey."

Samuel's head swivels away from the TV but focuses on nothing. Mouth hangs. He speaks words garbled and lost and he turns back.

"He okay?"

The man with the book shrugs.

"Maybe he hates his job," he says.

The man in the cap makes a noise like a word.

"Ha."

"And put that away," says the man with the book. "This is a neutral place."

The man in the cap laughs a genuine laugh but he slips the envelope away.

"You're a delight, Honest."

Honest turns a page in the book. The man in the cap wags a finger at bottles, at taps.

"What's cheap?"

The bargirl looks at Honest. Honest nods. She sets a chilled bottle in front of the man in the cap. Beer, domestic, something gold.

He takes off his cap and sets it on the bar. He talks and he laughs at something he himself says, goes on for minutes about the TV and the world. He sips and he drinks. He talks about the heat and about the coat Samuel wears in spite of weather and reason. Samuel hears his name and pours himself another glass of whatever the bottle holds. The man puts his cap back on and drinks and he peels a bill from the envelope as he stands. He sets the now empty bottle on top of the note and he rounds the bar, taps Samuel's arm. Samuel looks up, zeroes in on the other man. There is no recognition, and then there is.

"Carl."

"Morning, Sam."

The envelope is passed over and gone and the man, Carl, pulls at the brim of the hat as he eyes the bartender for only a moment, polite and off putting. He wrinkles his nose as he passes by the end of the bar, points a finger gun at Honest, mocking or not. The door opens and noise comes and he is gone, swallowed by the day. Samuel takes a drink. Honest turns a page. The bargirl changes the channel but there is nothing on.

2. Then

The hallway went on for a block, for miles, a haze of sun streaming in through unwashed glass and broken every few feet by a strip of darkness cast by a slip of wall separating each pane from the next, on and on for the expansive length of that carpeted, vacant sprawl. Voices existed behind doors, some booming, others shared in whispers, all laying out one edifying lecture or another with the rote professionalism of the experienced. Samuel moved alone through that corridor, in and out of the light, silent as he approached his destination. He was twelve years old and late for class.

Doe eyes in a dozen round faces turned to look as he pushed through the door. The sensation of something halted hung, a mouth ajar and the hint of echoed words perceived by the brain but not registered in any true or intelligible sense. A twang of instinct. Someone yawned.

A man stood behind a desk and faced the room. Older man, maybe an old man. Words crawled across a blackboard, one larger than the rest, circled in chalk. ALEX. He spoke.

"You'll need to make a decision."

Samuel took an empty seat. Heads faced front and Alex carried on with his lesson, a talk on a culture and society long left to dust. Youths would droop in seats or ask questions they hoped would please or they feigned interest while minds moved far away, and he offered response or discussion, engagement where it could be found. He spoke in practiced blocks of syllables, the expert clip and strict manner of a man with an unseen accent running just underneath the surface of every word and phrase. He asked the right questions and they would answer or they wouldn't and the day traveled along its track.

A bell rang. Heads turned and feet moved. Class was over and another would soon begin. Samuel waited. Alex read through a book at his desk, a worn collection of fairy tales, leather-bound and old, cover lettering stamped in German bold. As time went by the classroom emptied.

"Yes?" said Alex, not looking up from his book.

Samuel crossed the room.

"I wanted to apologize."

"You wanted to apologize."

"Yes."

"For what?"

"I was late."

"People are late every day," said Alex. He set the book down on the desk, page still open. A bare sketch of a screaming face stood out on the yellowed paper. Crooked teeth and hollow eyes, nothing there but endless void.

"What is that?"

Alex looked at the drawing, its dreadful rage captured forever in a few crude lines. He closed the book.

"Just a story," he said. "A fable about a demon."

3. Now

An alarm is buzzing and has been for some time. Afternoon light pours in slices through blinds. 1 o'clock, 2 o'clock. Samuel turns off the alarm without looking. He stumbles through a waking routine with eyes closed; brushing teeth, stretches, crunches. Hands splash water on face and the world begins to focus.

———

The priest comes on Mondays. He brings with him a shoebox. Sometimes he brings a satchel. The regulars part as he moves through the office park lobby. Pleasant face, vacant.

"Boys."

A word to no one in particular. Ever Collins watches with predatory glare. Floral buttondown, blue and insane. Three hundred pounds, easy. Samuel doesn't look up from the day's paper. Carl removes his cap. It's always the same, or it's close enough to the same. Hat chews ice from a dented Styrofoam cup, the gap separating his front teeth showing. Jeffries chats with the barista working the lobby counter about the weather, about the price of things.

"Hot enough?"

"Maybe it'll rain. Rain helps."

The priest takes the elevator and is gone. They watch him go, these castoffs, these faithless. Others mill about or they come and go. They drink sweet coffees with exotic names and they wait for jobs or for news of jobs. They exist.

The priest comes down and is gone in the same friendly void he at most times inhabits. James soon follows. Overpriced suit and haircut. He clears his throat.

"Is Lou Henry around?"

Jeffries turns and speaks without pulling up from the counter on which he leans, slouched and lounging.

"He might be at church."

A few chuckles, some awkward looks, and that same controlled menace in Ever Collins. James points at Carl.

"You."

He talks and Carl listens, accepts instructions with a blank understanding. Talk drones on and he nods. And.

"Sam. Go with him."

Curbside. Street traffic is light, the midday flow already arrived at its destination, evening's pedestrians not yet unleashed. Samuel holds a cigarette. No one that passes is smoking.

A woman stands on the sidewalk staring at the screen of a phone in her hand. She looks up, out at the street, waiting for a car or friend, hoping for some moment yet to come. Samuel looks in through the glass doors at a world he's only just stepped out of. Waiting.

"You can't smoke that in there."

Samuel turns.

"They used to keep ash cans out front," he says.

Her eyes narrow. He drops the cigarette in a plastic trash bin and steps off the curb. Carl sits behind the wheel of a cab up the block. Samuel gets in and inhales. Intense pine, cloying and aggressive. Air fresheners hang at strategic points. They pull into the street, join the sparse traffic ebb. The sun begins its fall from the sky.

———

Still time left. Hours to go. Carl mentions food and he's already wheeling into a lot as Samuel only nods and goes on watching the faces move by on the other side of the window. Shift to park. Carl looks around. He opens the glove box, he opens the console. Shuffling items. Napkins, papers. He comes up with a pill organizer. Days of the week. Pops the top and removes tablets, something yellow, something blue.

"Sorry."

He closes his eyes and dry-swallows pills. The click of throat is loud in the quiet of the car. They step out.

The diner is thick with hot odors, grease and salt and others impossible to decipher. The noises of consumption work the room.

Chatter circles and cutlery knocks against dishes. A man shouts for a refill. Somewhere a bell chimes and chimes again.

"Burger," says Carl. He turns to Samuel. "Burger?"

Shrug, nod. A woman with a pen moves between counters. She writes and she speaks and he doesn't order drinks but she brings them anyway. When food comes Carl takes off his cap.

The same golden light that spills through diner windows washes across even far corners under the soft throw of overheads. A warm place. A man writes on a newspaper spread before him. Crossword or jumble. Someone reads a letter and sips black coffee, the torn envelope on a table among the leavings of a meal. The electric buzz and beep of future now is present but subdued. Newspaper flutters, the sound of a memory. Samuel takes a bite of burger. Juices, grease and ketchup and some nameless spice, exotic in its mundanity. Familiar, missed. Gulp of drink, all sugar and bubbles. He wipes his mouth with wads of napkin.

Carl takes small bites. He leans to a man at the next counter seat. Conspiratorial musings. The man upends a flask into a mug of some steaming brew. Carl nods approval and he takes his time eating. The man with the flask finishes his cup and repeats the process and Carl laughs along with the man. They share a last private joke and the man drops a crumpled ten next to his cup now drained, still warm to the touch. He stumbles and lurches his way into the world. Carl snatches the bill from the counter and slips it away in a hip pocket of jeans outsized and worn before the waitress stops by. She asks if he needs a refill, if he needs anything at all. He tells her no, thank you. He puts his cap back on his head.

———

Carl punches buttons on the radio as he drives. He stops on a song, something full of piano and years. He talks over the song.

"Why did he send you with me?"

There is no answer and he doesn't need one. He talks or he hums along with the song. He turns up the radio. Home is somewhere hours from now. An idea of a place. Samuel gives up listening and only watches passing landmarks, lights and signs that look like any other, familiarity in nothing and everything. The song ends and another begins.

The building is a nondescript finger pointing skyward, a residential tower with no name out front. A number on a door and an attendant with no neck. Carl parks on the street.

Private words are traded with the goon at the entrance. Samuel stands away, does not hear. Carl turns and he smiles and Samuel follows. The front hall is carpeted in the gauche red of a brothel or gala. An elevator ride seems to go on for minutes. Another hall on what could be any floor, the same offensive carpet ending in a door with no number. There is an odor, a stink of things foul, an awful presence that smacks the senses. Samuel knocks and Carl knocks and they look at each other and wait. The door opens. The odor grows. Carl nods to a woman holding open the door and disappears into the throng.

Music fills the void between conversations passed as Samuel moves among unkind faces. Jaunty melody, something '20s or '30s. A couch divides the flow of wandering bodies, cushions wrapped in plush green felt. Partygoers stand or sit and they trade words, strange talk in obscure tongues. Carl migrates to a bookshelf. He runs a finger along undusted tomes. Leans in, squints at faded titles. He touches a book a second time but doesn't remove it from its place.

A man sits unblinking as the room moves all around. The cloth of his gaudy white suit is tailored to let breathe his thin frame. Something wrong with those eyes. Unsettling and odd. He grins wide and shows teeth and his smile is an unpleasant thing that follows Samuel, unchanged and curious.

Samuel pours a drink.

The bar is unmanned, lines of bottles and glasses and ice left alone and waiting. A man splashes seltzer over ice and the dregs of some brown fluid. He rubs a hand across the stubble of his scalp, the noise of its slow grating audible above the croon of some long dead songbird. The beard of a monk or a lunatic. Older man. Eyes that roll and weave and at times narrow. Mean, wild. Lou Henry. He sips and he speaks.

"Only a fool drinks at work."

Samuel shakes his glass, ice chiming its own pleasant tune. This is all he offers up as response.

Bodies move and they twirl, an incomprehensible dance, unorchestrated or so impossibly orchestrated as to be beyond understanding, the chaotic march of a billion tiny moments. All manner of dress, the finery among the tattered. Destructive libations are consumed by all. Chaos spreads. A figure unmoving for minutes or more stirs from his place on plush carpet and rises resurrected to the world. He looses a grunted syllable and grabs a drink from a table. He talks to no one and he nods along with his own voice. Careful steps carry him off in the direction of closed doors, a distant, unlit hall across the crowded room. Carl peels away from the lines of books to follow the stumbling wreckage into darkness. Lou Henry speaks.

"How do you feel?"

"About what?"

"You know what your friend is doing in the next room right now."

"I do."

"How does that track with you?"

"How does that track with me."

"What do you think about it?"

"Lou."

"Drink your drink. Take a minute."

"Well."

Samuel trails. He drinks his drink.

"James was looking for you."

"I'll bet," says Lou Henry.

A woman spills a drink. Someone gasps, someone laughs. The man in white goes on grinning and watching.

"That one finds it amusing you're here."

Samuel doesn't turn, knows who he means.

"What does he think of you?"

Hard glare, a hint of a smile.

"They don't know what to think of me."

Refills and escape. Samuel's glass is overfull, sloshing over lip of glass as he walks. No one seems to watch or care but that one unblinking, unsettling fiend.

The balcony is inhabited but quiet. Hushed talk of distant clusters, insignificant. Samuel takes a cigarette from the pack, holds it. He smells the tobacco, a sweet scent, like raisins but not. An ashtray sits on a ledge, wiped clean, unused. He turns his back on the world and looks instead to the room he's just left. Minutes pass and the vibrating mass of what looks like humanity but isn't plays its part. Shifting in place, moving and imitating with practiced near perfection the talk and the look and the personality quirks of people, real people, but underneath each mask of flesh is something awful, some unnamable horror. He takes a drink.

"You're really making that last."

She doesn't smell like the others, the taint of ruin absent. She smells earthy and pleasant, the smell of some memory, fresh cut grass. He looks at the unlit cigarette dangling from loose fingers, a forgotten bauble.

"They aren't cheap," he says.

"What do you do?"

"I'm a lawyer."

"Is that what you tell people?"

He shrugs.

"You look like you slept in those clothes."

"I did sleep in these clothes."

She looks at him. He looks at the room, its own world, spinning its way through the night on the other side of the glass.

"You know who I am," he says.

"I do."

A breeze cuts the moment, an inexplicable chill ignorant of the heat. Hair shifts under the touch of that draft, exposes her slender neck. A halo of loose strands swaying. He trembles. She only stands. He offers his coat. Her eyes close, her face tilting down. She shakes her head just once. The breeze passes and is gone. She turns to look beyond the ledge at the world below. He speaks.

"And what is it you do?"

"When?"

"Whenever."

Her smile is polite.

"I'm a lawyer."

Talk fades and in the room bare limbs and swaying hips shift and they yield as Carl works his way to the door and out. The man in white goes on grinning the grin of the mad as the long dead sing their songs on a stereo in another room. Samuel drinks his drink and long before the body in the bedroom is discovered he follows Carl into the night.

———

The world is empty. Streetlamps buzz or they don't, patches of light flickering along vacant streets under that electric hum. A vague blue touches the east, not yet day but no longer night. No cars pass. The party exists minutes or hours in the past, its attendants frozen in the amber of memory, forever captured in a moment.

A river runs beneath a bridge. Ground trembles at its rumbling passage. Someone jumps every few months, sometimes more. They drown or they sink, ribs shattered from impact, bodies shattered, souls shattered. Most are found washed up along the bank, others become ghosts, carted off to nowhere, vanished from the world.

Samuel looks into current passing underfoot, listens to the on-rush of unending flow for minutes or more, the world's own sigh. He closes his eyes. The world goes on breathing. It's morning.

4. Now

Air conditioning hums in overhead vents. A compressor kicks on and the building exhales. The coffeemaker emits a forbidding murmur and it drips and it pours. It speaks in sizzles and burns.

Carl stands under that cold breath. He holds a mug in two hands, blows across steam rising from the surface. Sugary swill, clutched, coveted. The compressor shifts gears. There's something alive in the walls and Carl can't feel his skin.

Samuel half awake pushes through the front door and into the office park lobby. Eyes rimmed in red blink and they stare uncomprehending. A sign is taped to the lacquered face of the bathroom door. OUT OF ORDER.

"Lobby can's busted up," says Hat.

An elevator opens. No one gets out.

Speakers are set into elevator walls but no song plays here. Samuel rides up and gets out and moves past doors that open onto disparate worlds, cubicle farms or chatting faces or a wide office space occupied by an old man on an ancient telephone at the room's only desk. Someone sells bibles over the internet. Signs mark their names, these pocket universes, nameplates on doors or walls.

Lavender bathroom. In and piss and out. Life pulses behind hallway doors. A voice speaks up as Samuel attempts his escape.

"Sam."

He stops in a doorway. No company name, no posted hours. A painting of some mad ancient stares wide eyed hate in a canvas hanging from one wall. Gaunt Euro skull, hair combed hard away from face, aristocratic and severe. Chipping in places. James sits behind a desk.

"Have you seen Jeffries?"

Samuel shakes his head.

"I can go by his place."

James says no and he has nothing else to say. Samuel enters the elevator. The doors close. A song begins to play.

A stooped and squinting patron waits at the bar for a drink but there is no one around to pour. Misty light streams in from the open back door, a haze of dust drifting on the air. A man eats a salad at a table scarred with strained poetry or the thoughtful musings of the long past. Something fries in a kitchen, the pop and sizzle of seared meat.

Samuel leans against the bar. He looks at the man waiting for a drink that won't come. The man turns to Samuel and then he turns away. Honest dips a paperback in mild hello.

"Drink?"

Samuel shrugs. Seconds fall off the clock. He rubs his face, his eyes, pushes the back of one hand against the lid, hard. He wipes forehead with a sleeve and reaches across the bar for a bottle of water from rows of them set up like bowling pins. Honest turns a page in his book.

"You sleep?"

Samuel wags a hand, noncommittal.

"Have you seen Jeffries?"

"Burgess might've."

"Where's he at?"

Honest points with the book toward the back door propped open and the buzzing, sighing world noise beyond.

Life is heard but not seen, an indigenous beast spinning and breathing in the distance, somewhere else, not here, all cars and talk and feet. Burgess holds a glass by the rim, dangling from fingers, interest losing, almost lost. Melted ice and something golden, layers upon layers. Small man in a check tweed suit, bowtie, wingtips polished, proud. He points down the alley.

"There was a horse."

"What?"

He looks over his shoulder at Samuel.

"Down the block. A horse wandering around on its own. There ought to be a law."

"What are you doing out here, Burgess?"

A sneer and a noise, naked scorn.

"The bathrooms in these places."

He goes on looking down the alley for a horse that might happen by, might not exist. He lifts the drink, sips from the lip of the glass. He nods.

"You want a drink?"

Each word is strung out in casual drawl, a momentary slip into an accent he tries to hide or one he on occasion feigns. Real or imaginary, faux Southern, a slow drip of syllables. Samuel doesn't respond for a long time. Then he does.

"Has Jeffries been around?"

Burgess sips and he speaks without turning.

"Is he missing?"

"I'm just asking."

"What are you asking?"

"James is looking for him."

"People go missing. You have to have the stomach for this work. Old fashioned zealotry to know the path you're on is the righteous one. The old German knew that. Him I liked. James pushes pencils."

"Burgess."

"Yeah."

"Have you seen Jeffries?"

"Tell James I want to talk to him."

"Tell him yourself."

Burgess turns again like he's going to speak but he doesn't speak. He grins and he points but the alley is still empty of movement or life and all that remains is a man with drink in hand standing among the aftermath of some nameless urban carnage. Samuel goes back inside. Honest speaks without looking up from his book.

"What's he doing out there?"

"He's taking a leak."

The man with the salad scans the room. The remains of his meal are a picked over wasteland. He looks for a take-out box or a trash bin. Fork pokes at a soggy leaf. He stands and leaves. Honest turns a page in his book. Samuel speaks.

"I'm looking for a Maggie."

The book dips. Honest licks a finger and bends a page to save his place. He shuts the book and looks Samuel in the face.

"What?"

"There was a Maggie at a thing."

"I heard about the thing."

"Know a Maggie?"

"I do."

"Well."

Scribbling in the paperback, the sound of paper tearing. Honest hands over numbers on a page. He shakes his head when he does it. He asks if Samuel wants a drink. Samuel's eyes wander across the bottles that line the shelf behind the bar. He sips water but his mouth remains dry.

———

The payphones are gone. He walks for three blocks, four blocks, turning corners at random in search of a booth or call box mounted to aging city brick. Pedestrians stagger past, sluggish under midday sun. They poke at handfuls of digital gadgets or they hold those devices out before them, each plugged into the same ephemeral dream, the faces of those passersby immersed in what flashes across tiny screens.

Five blocks, six.

Sidewalk shimmers in day heat. Store windows look in on little worlds. Old men with round bellies watch the street and the stream of life passing by. Breads are sold from a smiling silhouette in a darkened boutique. Homemade soaps are sold off a cart. Old shops, lost in time. Samuel enters a fast food hub, the only door with a familiar name.

"Do you have a phone?"

A waitress shrugs, another frowns. Samuel steps to a counter that comes to his neck and he points at a wooden panel above a bar where a chalkboard is nailed in place. Items are listed in faded colors. A handprint where someone wiped a word away. He orders a burger and coffee from a child with the wispy beginnings of a beard.

"You want ketchup?"

"No."

"We keep all the condiments under the counter. Otherwise the lurkers run off with everything."

"Okay."

"Napkins, too."

"I don't want any ketchup."

Food comes and he eats at a scratched wooden table, the names carved by staff. Manufactured character. A newspaper is left by someone now gone. Samuel holds the paper and he flips through pages. Local news, days old. His coffee is bitter and black. Steam rises from a hole in the lid of a Styrofoam cup. He sips and he reads with compulsive devotion every word detailing events now past. He takes a bite. He sets down the burger to chew and read more.

A door opens, a wheel squeaks. A cart cluttered with arcane baubles rolls between unbussed tables. Coats thick and thin, utilitarian articles clipped or hanging from bars inside and out, tools, all manner of bag. This wheeling amalgam of functional detritus makes its steady progression under hands filthy and jutting from a tattered white suit. Samuel grabs the man's frayed sleeve.

"You."

The man in white recoils. Hip bumps table and then cart and the racks of gathered miscellany rattle and clang as the works tilts and threatens to capsize but is righted once more by Samuel, half risen, wary.

"Sit with me."

The man in white tucks his cart between tables and stares with wide gray eyes first at Samuel and then at his burger. Samuel flags down a passing waitress and orders another of the same.

"Your eyes are different."

The man in white nods. A new plate is set before him. He nods again, accepting of the moment without committing or clarifying, only acknowledging that moments are passing, people are talking. They sit across from each other that way, silent, waiting in the den of this franchise eatery. A woman circles the room wrapped in a vest of aggressive yellow. A ponytail juts from a tan visor. De facto hostess. She asks if they need anything. She turns up her nose at the stink of the man in white, the transient, the bum. She does not look at this man. Samuel thanks her. He says they're fine. The bum closes his eyes until she moves on.

A bite into burger. He nods as he chews. He looks at the burger and at Samuel. He nods. Cheekbones strain at flesh. This skeletal wraith smiles as he eats. Samuel offers little and pushes fries around a tray and soon enough he pushes his own plate aside. He exhales and he leans back and the bum watches this as he chews.

"Who are you?"

The bum nods again. Hand dabs at grinning mouth with paper napkin. Mouth filled with food, poking out at the edges of that grin. Samuel watches with morbid fascination. The bum swallows and dabs a second time. That obscene smile disappears behind this gesture of rote civility. He folds the napkin and slips it into a pocket of that weathered suit coat. He sips at a sweating glass of carbonated something and he begins to speak, his voice a dry whisper, wind seeping through cracks, the parched sigh of a man's first words after untold silent years. He doesn't know how long he's been here, or he knows but the answer changes as he goes along. Sometimes he doesn't remember where he is. He uses names of places contradictory to reason and these he himself unsays as he goes on speaking with lucid, confident articulation.

A plug of a man in a tracksuit drops a massive cup to the floor. Ice crashes across tile, noise like feral applause. The man in white stands and with wide eyes runs for the door, leaving his carted collection of meager possessions behind. Samuel wipes hands on pants, on sleeves. He leaves a tip although no one else has. The circling waitress waves as he stands, she doesn't know why. He asks again to use their phone. The waitress frowns but she says okay.

"There's a payphone by the bathrooms."

Maggie. Samuel flattens the paper and runs a finger across the line of numbers. A coin clanks its way through the phone's works and another follows the first. A child watches, turned around in a booth. Samuel looks away. The phone clicks and someone is there.

"Yes?"

Thick with sleep, sultry and feminine. Scrape of cloth on phone as she touches her face, wipes away a dream now gone.

"Who is this?"

Samuel folds the page from the paperback. He slips the paper away in the pocket from which it came. The line goes dead.

He looks at the phone in his hand and at the base on the wall. He plugs in more coins.

He calls and she answers and he says little. She asks who it is and he says it's the lawyer and she says she knows. She agrees to meet for drinks and she says her name is Maggie and he doesn't say anything. A man turns in his booth and knocks on the glass. He looks around to see if anyone else is looking.

"That's a goddamn horse."

He points and he says it a second time. A horse ashen of coat stands statue still in the lot. Dreamlike, carved in the moment. Seconds pass. It turns and looks with black orb eyes at the men staring spellbound through windows uncleaned in months or more. It takes each step without hurry and at the street no car passes or even appears as the horse turns and is gone.

———

Music drowns the room in the crash of its tide. Faces lean close at tables, in booths, strangers with lips moving slow against ears, making even the most casual toss of words something secret, sacred.

She knows this place. The stumbling lost and their shouting and touching, their singing along with the song playing or another entirely, their groping and madness and the chaotic press of humanity all around. She knows this place. She's there with a drink when he walks through the door.

The pale waif bartender leans across the bar. Curls veil eyes. She speaks words lost in the din and she points, but Samuel is already there. He slaps the bar with a flat palm. Heads turn, but not many.

"Sam," he says.

She leans in to speak over noise and bodies and bass and sweat.

"I know."

The bartender puts a glass in front of Samuel. She says something but no one hears and she moves away. Honest watches over the top of his book. He licks a finger and turns a page and pretends he does not see.

"You were at the party," says Samuel.

"Yes."

"At their party."

"So were you," she says.

He takes a drink. He looks at her and takes another. Ice rattles in the bottom of a glass. The bartender leans across the stained wood block to pour him a fresh one and top off hers. Maggie sips and she speaks again.

"What are you asking me?"

He touches the question, tastes it and all it holds. His chin begins to lower and for a moment he's far away.

"There was this man today. Before I called you."

"What man?"

"Guy in a suit. White suit, nice, or it used to be. One of them, but not like them. He was there the other night. He had these strange eyes at the party, but today they were just eyes. Today he was different."

Lips purse and nostrils flare.

"Oh. Him."

She finishes her drink and waves for a refill. Samuel sees the empty and downs his in a gulp in time for the bargirl to replace it with another. Conversation relaxes, or it pretends to. He smiles and he asks questions she doesn't answer and he drinks. He drifts past further mention of work and she does the same. He drinks and she sips and they bask in the feigned normalcy of it all. He drinks and they trade casual talk on anything at all. She watches the door, the room. He drinks. Eyes grow dull and jaw protrudes. He stares hard at nothing.

"Come home with me."

"Is that why you called me?"

"No."

"Why did you call me?"

"Come home with me."

She drinks her drink and she orders another. Cold liquor sloshes past the lip of an overfilled glass to spill across elegant legs. The room spins and music thumps hard against bodies. Samuel inhales thick, hot air. Booze and sweat and fresh cut grass and the smell of her is wild.

————

The knock is an insignificant thing, a dull tap against a door in some other world. It comes again, now hard, a fist crashing with force, a thud that is felt as much heard. Samuel opens his eyes but the world remains steeped in darkness. He pulls on clothes and mumbles pale words to the owner of that knock, an ineffectual consolation thrown into shadow, no way to know if its intended recipient either hears or accepts.

Light seeps in as he cracks open the door.

"James."

The suit is gaudy but immaculate, every stitch of its silver frame perfect, sewn by the tiny hands of some obsessive maniac with the love of finery but no taste at all.

"Open up."

A sliver of space grows, through which James slips with a flourished step. The door closes. Both men disappear into the darkness.

Shuffling in the dark. James follows the sound of bare feet on wood floor. When a light pops on the two men are in a half kitchen. Stove light, weak and yellow. A wall separates the little room from the apartment proper. Samuel sets a coffeepot in the sink and turns on the tap. Water spills over the sides. He runs a wet hand across his face. The water is cool in the heat of the room. Head pounds as liquor burns through veins. He puts the pot into the maker.

"What time is it?"

"You stink," says James.

Samuel waves a hand in the air, dismisses the idea of this. James goes on.

"It's late."

"You want coffee?"

"No."

Samuel scoops coffee into a filter. He pushes buttons until the maker emits a satisfying coo. James goes on.

"He never showed up."

"Jeffries?"

No response.

"Means nothing. People disappear every day. They go to jail, they skip town. People go away. It's one guy. It means nothing."

"Three guys."

"Who else?"

"Nobody. Burgess' guys."

Samuel pours coffee from the pot into a mug. He stands holding the cup in two hands but he does not drink. Liquid sizzles as the dregs in the maker drip onto the heating element.

"I saw Burgess today. He didn't say anything about it."

"Go see Lou Henry," says James.

"You think it's him?"

A shrug.

"You think it's him."

"I hope it's him. It's easier if it's him. Talk to Lou Henry."

Old mugs sit forgotten by the sink. Scum rings their lips. Samuel looks into the swirling black. He pours the coffee down the sink and leaves the mug with the others.

"I'll ask around."

"Don't ask around. Talk to Lou Henry. If it's the other side, I want to know it's the other side, but first I want to know if it's him."

James slips into the darkness. Footsteps trail through the room. His voice comes from far away.

"Carl will be outside when you come down in the morning."

"What time?"

Light leaks into the room, a line of clarity defining existence alongside that dense, impenetrable black.

"When you come down," says James.

The door closes and the world beyond the kitchen disappears. Samuel turns a knob on the stove. A burner clicks and blue fire reaches for the heavens. A pack of cigarettes wait in pants pocket. He pulls one, plugs his mouth, leans into the fire. Smoke fills lungs. He turns off the burner.

The bed sags under his weight. He shifts and he moves. Back presses to wall. Ember glows hot as he inhales. Thin light appears in the dark. Maggie checking phone. A pale face where it meets that cold light's touch. Words scroll and slip away. She presses a button and the light is gone. Her voice is a soft caress in the void.

"So you do smoke those."

He tips ash in a tray beside the bed. She puts out a hand. He passes the cigarette over. She puts it to soft lips and breathes.

"That was my employer."

"I know."

"You know a lot."

She passes back the cigarette.

"No one knows a lot," she says.

5. Then

The phone never stopped ringing. Lines would light up, a flickering orange square that pulsed to the beat of the ring. Samuel sat at a desk and answered the phone and when he would hang up it would ring again. Sometimes he would transfer a call to a back office where Alex sat or where he paced in the dark. Most calls he turned away. He was twenty years old and he had no idea what his boss did for a living.

Men would arrive and they would speak with Alex, shared words in hushed tones. They spoke and Alex nodded and these men would go off to do some task. Samuel watched them go and he asked no questions. These strangers did not look at him. Roughneck thugs with knuckles that dragged. The phone rang and he answered it.

Some nights Alex didn't leave. He would lock the door to the inner office and walk in circles, working over a notion, picking it to pieces and putting it back together, a puzzle of thought. Samuel stayed on those nights. He answered the phone or he sat and he waited. He read the paper. It was always the same story, some twist on old news.

It was late, it was some unknown hour, that dead, desolate moment existing miles from anything civil. Samuel flipped through comic strips geared to some other generation. He folded the paper over and for a moment he was lost in the sound it made, a noise that spoke to some primal thing. He unfolded the pages and folded them again but it wasn't the same.

A bell chimed over a door and it left a man standing on the square of tile that marked the entryway. His head moved in circles, trying to pop a vertebrae or maybe something else, a string cut, the works unmoored. His suit hung loose on thin limbs, fit like it belonged to someone else. Jacket flapped open. Blood soaked the shirt underneath. He walked to the inner office and shut the door behind him. The bolt snapped shut.

They talked and they shouted, some in English, some not. Alex cursed in German. The cursing Samuel could follow, the rest only a garbled disarray. He looked at his paper but he didn't go back to reading. He looked at the main door but didn't leave. The talk went on.

There was a silence that spread out in time, a pool of nothing that cramped stomach, clutched heart, a well of minutes in which anything could happen, everything could be wrong. Something needed done, some action to settle the growing dread that rested upon the room, but Samuel sat and he waited. He did nothing. He did not know what to do.

The bolt snapped open. The door soon followed.

Muttering leaked from the inner office. Words existed in that noise, juts of lucidity in an amorphous hum. That murmur cut off. The man left the inner office. He nodded at Samuel as he walked by and out.

Alex grunted. He cleared his throat and sighed. As he left the inner office he dragged a chair behind. A grating sound. He stopped and he sat by Samuel's desk, back straight, hands clasped on the wood surface. Polite, prim.

"Do you know that man?"

Samuel shrugged.

"He's been in before. I've seen him a few times."

"He works with me. Tell me what you saw."

"What?"

"That man."

A shake of head. Nonchalance.

"Nothing important."

"That's good. That's correct. Why?"

"He's no business of mine."

Alex waited. Crags and trenches divided the flesh of his face, lines worn through time. His age asserted itself in the silence. All the cold the years had earned, the hard emptiness that hid behind eyes. He waited in that cold.

"Correct," he said. He inhaled, exhaled. Hands untangled and fingers drummed just once along the desk. They righted themselves, each digit interweaving with its counterpart once more. He went on.

"Have you seen death?"

"I don't know what that means."

"A man died in front of me. In the snow, years back. He looked at me and he told me things. He was a wicked man, he said. He'd lived a wicked life. He laid there bleeding and he asked me what he should do."

"What happened?"

"He died."

A pause landed and grew. Samuel blinked, waited. Alex was stone. Samuel broke.

"I don't know what you want me to say."

Alex's face changed, a slight shift in something underneath the skin. Hand drummed on desk. Face stared at hand, eyes loose, someplace far away chasing the tendrils of evasive thought. Hand stopped, pupils focused. He spoke.

"Sam, where do you see yourself in five years?"

It went on this way, their talk did, that ersatz interview, but the phone never once rang and Samuel already had the job.

6. Now

No one is up, no one is out. The drunks have scurried out of sight and the office crowd is still sleeping. A blue veil spreads across the first minutes of dawn. The day's inhabitants begin to appear, a jogger passing in a hurry to nowhere or the bleary eyes of a walker attached to a dog. Lights turn from red to green and back again with no one waiting, no one to go or to care.

A car waits at the curb, an idling Checker taxi, dented and archaic. Carl sits behind the wheel digging through a pill organizer. He tosses a pill out the window and then he tosses another. Something yellow, something green. He doesn't look up as Samuel gets in back.

"Some weather, yeah?"

Chin to chest as he speaks, face down, eyes on the contents of the pill case.

"Let's go, Carl."

Carl's eyes find Samuel in the mirror.

"In a hurry to get it done? Yeah. I would be, too."

The lid of each day of the week is clasped in a crisp succession of pops. Foot on brake and car in gear. He sits that way, engine rumbling. He plays with the radio. Faceless strangers talk about the state of society. He looks at the radio like it's talking to him and him alone. Seconds pass. He nods at nothing in particular and the car begins to move.

The radio talks and no one else. City streets pass by, block after block of life beginning to stir behind windows, behind walls. Streetlamps buzz where they've not yet gone dark. A woman jogs in place on a sidewalk. The cab keeps moving.

The building was once a bank. Now its grand interior is bisected with walls and spackle and pedestrian function. Apartments, all. A monolith of concrete and stone, alien among surrounding city modernity. A slender front hides the structure's size. The side runs the length of the block. A clock sits bolted to the building's face with hands stilled by time. A mouth of a door is frozen in scream. Samuel looks out the open cab window and down that gullet. A shudder runs through the car as transmission shifts past gear after gear until it settles into park. Carl eyes the mirror.

"You want me to do it?"

Samuel pulls his gaze back from the mouth of the building.

"This one's just a conversation."

Those eyes move away from the mirror. He turns up the radio. Voices talk traffic. A highway is shut down somewhere.

"Suit yourself."

Samuel steps out of the car.

Steam rises from a grate, an escaped breath from some mad hell. A man reaches out, touches Samuel's arm.

"Warm this morning."

Samuel slows but doesn't stop. The man smiles. He's clothed in rags once fine, once holy. Crumbling vestments of the ordained. Scars for eyes, old flesh hardened. Face unshaven. He runs a hand across his own cheek and he speaks of God in all His glory. He asks for a dollar, for a donation to the ministry. The face of that eyeless street preacher turns and it follows Samuel's progress as he moves along sidewalk and into the building's gaping scream.

Footsteps clap on tile. Twenty-somethings linger in doorways trading opinions and making noise. Already awake or still awake. A laughing voice asks a question as Samuel passes. He does not stop. He does not respond.

There is no elevator. Stairs lead up past echoes of the lobby, halls and doors and more of the same. First floor voices drift up along the stairwell, but each floor now passed sits in cold silence save the tap of those footfalls as they make their ascent.

A door waits where stairs end. He knocks and a voice speaks from somewhere within the world it hides. Unintelligible words. He turns the knob and no one stops him from entering, no bolts or locks barring his way.

"Look who it is."

Lou Henry's voice is a toneless thing, frank and bored. He sits in a worn office chair stolen or found, maybe left behind in these ruins when the bank vacated years ago, decades ago. One laced boot hangs suspended at the end of a leg draped over a knee, casual. Another man sits on a couch against one wall. He writes in a notebook and does not look up. Round glasses magnify eyes, their thin wire frames wrapped around small ears. Samuel waits for Lou Henry to introduce the bespectacled man but no introduction comes.

"Have a seat."

"I'm not staying."

"Well then."

He offers Samuel a drink and he laughs. Samuel says nothing. The bespectacled man goes on writing. Pen scratches paper. This is the only sound for seconds.

"James send you here to shoot me?"

Samuel says nothing.

"Why are you here?"

"Some guys have gone missing."

Lou Henry uncrosses his legs. He sits forward, elbows on knees, hands hanging low.

"Of course they have. These are not righteous men."

Samuel circles the room in a cavalier stroll. He studies with feigned interest the sparse furnishings and hollowed framework of what once was a corner office. A crucifix hangs on one wall, Elvis nailed to the cross.

"That a confession, Lou?"

"Maybe they're being punished by God. Maybe they're being spirited away. The Lord's loyal servants, raptured one at a time."

The grate of pen on paper is loud in the room.

"Who's he?" asks Samuel.

"Don't mind him. He's a scribe collecting my tale. My very own apostle."

The pen ceases its crawl. Its owner looks up at the room. He takes off his glasses and rubs palms against eyes. Maybe he speaks, no one hears. He puts the glasses on once more, loops wire around ear. The bespectacled man turns a page. He begins to write once more.

Lou Henry interrupts the silence.

"What do you want?"

"James wants to know if it's you."

"Your missing guys?"

Samuel doesn't speak, only waits.

"Why me? Why not the other side?"

Samuel shrugs.

"I don't care."

"Where's James? I want to talk to someone who does care."

The bespectacled man licks the end of his pen. The sound is a grotesque scraping. He goes back to writing, maybe what is being said or the broad strokes, the tone of the room, maybe something else altogether, some other event barely remembered or fabricated entirely.

"What do you think happens when they die?"

Samuel stops his slow circuit of the room.

"Who?"

"Them. The other side. Do you think they go to some literal netherworld of fire or do they simply cease to be? Do you think they even are the unimaginable monsters we've been told? What if they're just unwashed nobodies, obstacles in the way of whatever faceless exec sits in the big chair these days?"

Samuel pulls a pack of cigarettes from a pocket. He holds it out. Lou Henry frowns. Samuel, looks at it, waits, puts it back.

"Does it matter?"

Lou Henry claps once, hard, sits back in his chair.

"That's the spirit," he says.

Wild beard splays out from his otherwise hairless skull, jaw jutting beneath like the face of some ersatz revolutionary. He crosses legs once again and he goes on speaking.

"Maybe you're psychotic. Maybe none of this is real. Wouldn't that be something."

———

Platters of baked goods are spread across the table. Tea steams in cups. A plant acts as centerpiece, something green with leaves that hang low, slight browning where corruption sets in. Goons loiter; Ever Collins by the front hall, Samuel under the arch that separates the dining room from the kitchen. James sits at the table. He picks at a broken cookie and he chews. He checks a watch, a glittering work of gears and pomp endlessly ticking away.

A phone rings. Ever picks up the handset and offers unintelligible muttering. He drops the handset on its cradle and hooks a thumb at the door.

"Carl will be here with him in a minute."

He grabs a stack of peanut butter snacks from the table and disappears down the front hall. Soft murmur of boot on carpet. A door opens and shuts.

James drums fingers on table. He chews and he sips water. He speaks.

"Scale of one to ten."

"What."

"Odds are it's him, scale of one to ten."

"What number means we're sure enough to shoot him?"

James' answer is immediate.

"Seven."

"Six. He's at six."

"Six?"

"Yeah."

"That's close."

"Not close enough to kill him," says Samuel, and after a moment, "He found religion."

James fans the air, swats away the point.

"Lou was always a nut."

He trails off, stares into treats adorned with cubes of chocolate or coconut chunks, but whatever answer he is looking for is not found there.

Ever lurks on the front stoop. Lip curls in a grin of earnest contempt he does not know is showing. Hard eyes look right, look left, taking in the street, taking it apart a piece at a time. Empty houses hide behind uncut lawns all down the block, foreclosed or unsold parodies of homes. A suburban apocalypse, bereft of life. The street comes to an abrupt end at a field of nameless wild grass swaying in muted breeze. Chest high, maybe higher.

The cab is heard before it is seen, the chug of an old motor clinging with defiance to some kind of life, snarling with open menace as it guns through empty streets. Ever bites into a cookie and grinds it to mush between teeth as the ancient cab pulls to the curb. Backdoor opens with a groan. Lou Henry steps worn and cracking boots onto sidewalk. He straightens a tie as he moves up the walk. Carl waves from the cab driver's seat. The radio warns of coming dread. Ever sidearms a jagged chunk of cookie into whatever lies beyond the street's end. The sun begins to fall behind the world.

The men nod at each other as Lou files in. James wears a smile on an otherwise placid face.

"Fancy meeting you here."

"Where?"

"This is my home," says James, gesturing an open hand around to take in walls undecorated, cheap furniture set at odd angles in wide open spaces. "Got it for a steal. Pennies on the dollar."

"When empires fall even peasants can live like kings."

James grins with broad teeth, pearl, store bought.

"Is that the kind of conversation we're going to have?"

Lou Henry says nothing.

"Lou, I haven't been a peasant for ages."

More nothing. The amiable facade falls away from James. It happens all at once, a physical change, shoulders straight, face hard. He goes on.

"You requested an audience and here you stand. State your business, Lou."

"I came to see you."

"Yes. You did."

"At your office. Before things got rolling. I tried to warn you."

"No one's seen you in days."

"I tried once and here I am a second time," says Lou Henry. "You've been lied to. You damn yourselves in service to a false god."

"We were never pious men."

"You're not men at all. Psychopaths and mental patients. Idolaters. Charlatans."

"You sound like a crazy person."

"You sound like a car salesman."

Seconds play out. The room fills with time. Hard eyes soften as something creeps in. James leans back an inch. He points at the platters of confections in all their many forms.

"Sit. Eat something."

"No, thank you."

"A drink. A coffee."

Lou Henry pulls a chair away from the table. A slow whine of wood on tile cuts the quiet. He sits against the table's edge, hands out front, fingers splayed before him. He speaks one word.

"Coffee."

"Sam," says James.

Samuel steps into the kitchen. Weak light falls. He doesn't know where the switch is and he doesn't look. Talk goes on, a cryptic exchange that helps no one, solves nothing. He tunes out the noise, loses himself in the mundane. The bittersweet perfume of some exotic blend fills the room as he breaks the seal on a canister tucked among others. Unreadable label, words foreign, their letters arranged with whimsical flair. He leans down, inhales that earthy fragrance. Eyes roll back, fall closed and he is gone, someplace else, a primal place without name. He breathes out and in again but the moment is gone. He digs around for the scoop.

The first shot is a pop, sound softened by walls. Outside. Samuel jumps, blinks. Adrenaline slams. He drops the coffee. The second and third shot soon follow. After that he loses count. One final pop brings the world back into focus.

The dining room has emptied before Samuel moves through. Chairs stand away from each end of the table. Drops of water reflect light where they've splashed when someone slammed down a glass. A cookie half eaten sits alone on the table surface.

Silent steps move down the hall. Carpet eats noise. The front door stands open but only just. A loafer is visible on the stoop, the leg it belongs to trailing off, blocked by wall. Someone sprawls further along the walk, leaning back, resting on hands. Samuel pulls the door wide.

Blood soaks Ever's shirt. Wild splotches of its vaguely floral pattern are lost in that intense red. One foot digs at the concrete, a slow scrape, back and forth, doing nothing. The hole in his face pumps out life. His mouth works but no words are formed. Samuel steps over the leg.

Cab door stands open. Pebbles of glass dot the sidewalk, the grass surrounding. Carl's eyes are wide. He sits, feet kicking, lounging on sidewalk, one scuffed sneaker left behind where he scooted back on hands, four feet, five feet. He grins and looks around, nods without reason. A gun lies in the grass by one hand.

"How are you not hit?" asks Samuel.

Carl frowns down at himself.

"Am I not hit?"

James stands facing the open field, hands in pockets, turned away from the gathered ruin at his back. Grass doesn't move. Nothing moves. His voice is the only thing alive in the void of night.

"Is Lou in the house?"

Samuel looks back at the door and the empty hallway beyond. He shakes his head but does not speak. Wind kicks up. Grasses dance in that place at the end of the world. James' collar catches the gust, turns up at his neck. He takes a hand from his pocket and holds the fabric in place until the moment has passed.

———

Office park. The AC is off and smoke drifts in the hot, dead air. Blood trails off across acres of hallway carpet. Fibers dry and stiffen. Someone will come with a steamer, tomorrow, next week, some oblivious cleaning crew stuffed with men who won't ask and don't care. Until then the office park is closed.

Carl's leg hops in place. Just the one, the left. Right leg rests. An intensity, something too alive and wired wrong moves about behind his features. Wide eyes search without purpose. Something like a smile at times begins to form before falling in on itself. He looks at Samuel's back as Samuel stares out at the empty street beyond the office park turn-in, smoke rising from the ember of a forgotten cigarette at the end of one hand.

"Did you see him?"

"See who?"

"The phantom."

Time passes in the rise of smoke. Samuel looks over his shoulder as he speaks.

"What does that mean?"

He talks for five minutes, Carl does, doubling back on points, correcting himself or erasing thoughts, wiping them away and sculpting them again from the wreckage left behind. Samuel puts out a cigarette and lights another and listens to it all.

———

A song plays in the elevator, something old, wild, all trumpets and drums. A bell chimes and doors open and Samuel steps out. Ringing phones and chatting mouths and the reverberating noise of day life are all absent and only the song that before was silent now wanders these halls at his back.

The blood has changed. It's droplets here, not streaks, and soon it trails off to nothing. A lone handprint marks one wall. James' door stands open. A light is on and a laptop hums but the room is empty. Samuel touches the vinyl back of one chair but he does not sit. The music goes on, the same song or another just like it.

Doors are locked or they open on rooms perverted by their lack of bustling daytime components, the doomed souls of this place now exorcised and the shell left behind made unrecognizable by the stark metamorphosis.

He finds Ever in a break room. Cabinets are labeled with company names, each space divided up, claimed by one or another of the building's inhabitants. Muck gathers in adhesive left behind where old labels have been ripped away and replaced with new.

A bottle of whiskey sits on a table, its contents half gone, soaked into the towel pressed hard against the hole in Ever's face where an eye used to be. Soaking his shirt, soaking the man. A fury burns in the remaining eye staring hard at Samuel standing in the doorway. That eye is aware, clear even as the man it belongs to sways in his seat, pallid and slackjawed.

Samuel turns away.

The hall is no longer empty. James walks with head down, phone pressed to one ear. He talks and he listens. He points toward the elevator and doesn't slow. Samuel falls into step.

The doors close and the song rises. It is a living thing, seeping into every crevice, filling and consuming. James puts a hand over the open ear. Samuel stares at the speaker.

James hangs up without saying goodbye. The elevator doors open on the front hall, the foyer. Samuel tells the story just the way Carl told it to him. A man walked out of the night on sneakers. Sneakers, Carl swears, though he didn't know it then, not until after. The man spoke but the words were lost. A pale chin stuck out from a hood but the face was all shadow. He fired rounds into the door. Windows fractured or smashed. Carl popped his door and flopped back on pavement. He was shooting and the man was shooting and running both and somewhere the front door opened. Ever was struck and he was down.

"The phantom was gone."

Carl called him that then and he does so again now, cutting into the talk, staring off at nothing.

"He walked on sneakers. I only saw them at the end, as he was running for the field."

Carl starts in again, finding his place in the story, but it's told and retold and no one is listening. Calls are made, hushed affairs that clarify little. Men come and they go, some familiar, solemn individuals with guns bulging under coats. James' guys, part timers, others. Someone calls to say Burgess was shot at. The story is the same, or near enough. Men fan out across the city, into holes and hovels. Doors are kicked in. James goes up to his office, comes back. Carl calms and slumps and he sleeps across a row of lobby chairs. Someone goes to check on Ever. He doesn't move but he is not dead.

———

He doesn't know the time. It's day, the sun is up. Midday, maybe 9. He stumbles out of a cab in a daze. He doesn't remember the last time he slept real sleep. He moves up stairs and around a corner and up more stairs with no memory of the moment before, pristine in the oblivion of honest exhaustion. He steps out on a floor, his, walks with hand on wall to the door festooned with numbers that mean home or something like it. He puts in a key but the bolt is open. He turns the knob and enters.

She's there, Maggie is. She never left or she left and came back and he wants to ask which but his mind is a jumble of words. Ignorant of any reason at all. A numb mouth opens to say something, he knows not what, but a warm hand is pressed to his cheek and the broken puzzle of his thoughts is wiped away.

"You poor thing."

Her voice is a caress, a slow pressure that leaves him undone. He folds. She lets him. He collapses on the bed and in seconds is gone.

7. Now

No one knows a thing. Tips lead to nothing and soon they stop coming. The office in the bank building is emptied, the door left ajar. The crucified Elvis is left behind on the floor. A name is scrawled on one wall by some halfhearted vandal. A girl's name, no one important. Maybe the artist will bring her here, will point with a dull hope at the spot where her name is etched in a dripping, colorless font, but for now there is no hope in this place.

The blind street preacher in his sanctified rags touches the hands of passing sinners. He asks for nothing and from some he receives nothing, from others a dollar or a word. He thanks them, he blesses them. He shrinks as Samuel passes his perch on the sidewalk.

James doesn't leave the office park and soon he's not leaving his office. Takeout bags accumulate in a trash bin someone's dragged in and left by the door. No one empties it and the stink of rot grows. He opens his door and looks out, down one hall and then another. He stares at the elevator and waits. He never leaves, or if he leaves he doesn't go far.

Ever Collins is a ghost heard through walls, felt but not seen. He sleeps in an office belonging to no one and he haunts rooms thick with dust from months or years. Items are left for him, plates of food or pills in opaque, unlabeled bottles. The call center makes its calls and the little man in the room alone with his ancient rotary phone goes on living out whatever secret envelops his world and no one mentions the horrors that exist around corners and behind doors. Weeks vanish in dust. Samuel buys cigarettes by the carton.

The bar is populated with the day drunk, these sheepish patrons who down heavy pours with wide eyes and watch the room for a swift judgment that isn't there, doesn't come. They pull away as light invades, squinting, arms over faces. They remain wary long after the door has again shut out day.

Samuel sits and orders. Flick of hand and a gesture at a bottle, casual, done it a thousand times before. The bargirl pours. Honest licks a finger and turns a page in a paperback.

Burgess lounges on a stool. Shined Oxfords rest on a rail that runs along just above the ground. He leans full on the bar, craning toward bottles, toward mirror. Charm falls from his mouth, words curved at the edges in slight southern drawl. The bargirl talks back, pours tall shots of a greasy liquor that he sips between words. A tumbler of something thin sits untouched at his elbow. Orange peel hangs over the lip of the glass.

A finger from Samuel's drink hand extends to point at the man.

"Is he drunk?"

Honest doesn't look up from his book.

"He's not sober," he says.

The red, tired eyes of strangers follow Samuel as he rounds the bar and slides in beside the man.

"Hello, Burgess."

The man makes no eye contact, looks only into a drink poured in the same soiled glass he's been drinking from for hours or days. Burgess. He waggles a finger for refill at the passing bargirl. She nods like they're old friends with old routines.

"Well, but don't you just look like hell," says Burgess. "Sit. Drink with me."

He does. Glasses are sipped and topped off and sipped again. The bargirl makes light jokes about frivolous things, a touch of something familiar before she evaporates, whisked away by the world. Burgess rips a hole in the moment.

"Ever dead yet?"

"Not that I've heard."

Burgess holds up the tall shot. He holds the drink inches from his face, looks into swirling liquor as if some meaning resides in that black oil canvas.

"Good for him," he says. He downs the drink.

"Where's Lou Henry?"

Burgess snorts.

"Is he missing, too?"

Samuel says nothing. Burgess shrugs.

"Haven't found him. His scribe wandered into my orbit. Little guy with a notebook. I put some guys on him. Lost him. Life's like that."

"You think he did it."

Not a question.

"He ran," says Burgess, and then, "He'll turn up."

Light cuts once more through the room. Samuel cringes along with the rest of them. A man walks down and down and the dark returns, welcomes him to this place. He leans and speaks into Burgess' ear and what is said is only for him. Burgess nods and says two words, three words. The man looks past Burgess at Samuel. Burgess leans into his eye line.

"Hey. Go."

The man's gaze stays a moment longer until he finds he can pull away from a primal loathing he does not understand. He turns and walks into the light.

———

It's evening, it's night. The sun has fallen and Samuel walks until the hour is impossible to guess. Lights buzz over city streets and somewhere a car horn bleats rage and falls silent. He weaves a loose course toward his building but some turns lead away, make no sense. He pulls his coat around him and does not notice the heat.

The city is a maze. Pedestrians move about, lost within walls of steel and glass, stone towers that reach to a sky offering back only indifference. Glazed eyes look about at their surroundings and fail to see that they are lost. Samuel watches these drifting bodies. He sees only faces, strangers. Time passes and the civilized drift away in ones and twos, slipping into secret places. Businesses are closed and empty storefronts appear at random and the extras of the world are scattered, not here. The world has shut down for the night or it has gone dark forever. The twists of the labyrinth deposit Samuel at the door of the building he thinks of as home. He climbs stairs.

He looks at his boots, clings to the thud of each footfall that marks an unyielding progression toward some unknowable fate. He loses himself in that unremitting procession of steps and does not see the child until he is there, a step below the boy, the path blocked. The child faces Samuel with eyes that swim in a mad, infinite black. The boy smiles.

"Come to the roof," it says, that voice ruined, devoid of all that is human. "You should see this."

Samuel looks over his shoulder as he ascends and those pools of abyssal intelligence follow along until he rounds the corner and is free of their bleak appraisal.

The door to the roof stands open, night leaking in. The latch is bent out and useless from a kick dealt by some other man in some other time. City glow deadens the brilliance of countless stars. An aggressive silence hovers. Samuel hesitates at the door.

The man in white is on the ledge, face upturned to night. He moves his hands, pointing and pointing again, the suggestion of a symphony conducted that he alone can hear. Samuel lights a cigarette and waits. The man in white turns.

"Come look."

Samuel crosses the roof in short steps, no hurry in him. He breathes smoke and looks up but all that he sees is sky. Hands rest on ledge. The surface is warm. All about stand monuments to old worlds and new. Life glows in the windows of the temples of forgotten gods, worlds built upon worlds, some ruined, some not. The man in white looks past it all. He gestures again at the enormity of the vastness above. He turns those mad, swirling eyes upon Samuel to make certain he is seeing, turns back.

"Tell me what you see."

Smoke drifts from nostrils. Samuel taps ash over the ledge and onto the world.

"Stars, sky. I see night."

An audible sigh leaks from the man in white. He shakes his head without turning from the sky.

"No."

"I don't know what you want me to say."

The man in white turns again. He bends down, face just over

Samuel's, one arm flung out at his back, aimed at whatever lies above.

"It's the past. Everything you see has already happened."

Those knowing voids wait and they stay, holding the moment, expecting some understanding that does not come. Samuel looks up. He inhales smoke. The man in white turns back to the night sky.

"That light has traveled for millions of years, billions of years. That light is long dead and gone. What you see is the afterimage of hope."

What he sees is stars. Innumerable worlds formed under impossible odds. What he sees is the potential of a universe he does not understand, but he smokes and he says nothing.

"Someday eyes will look to those heavens and see nothing but black eons that go on forever. Look. Imagine it."

Samuel smokes. He pinches the filter between fingers and flicks it into city streets below. He tastes the burning air in mouth, lungs. Smoke leaks from nostrils like the only just contained fury of some fabled dragon. He exhales and he wants another. He remembers what life was like before he took up smoking again.

———

The stairs are clear, the child is gone. Samuel keeps hand on rail as he descends. He takes the steps two at a time. Nothing else moves. He reaches his floor, moves through the hall. Voices howl behind walls. Man and woman. He forgot. She didn't listen. They shout their secret rage for the world. Samuel enters his apartment but the noise is only dulled, not gone.

Springs ache, groan. The shape of a body moves under covers. The rise and fall of breath. Maggie. She comes and goes at will. Maybe she has her own key. Samuel doesn't know and hasn't asked.

The bathroom light is on, a sterile, petulant thing. Samuel leans across the sink. He pulls down at the flesh below one eye and bends close to the mirror.

"What are you doing?"

He doesn't hear her approach. She stands in the doorway as if she's always been there.

"Just looking," he says.

He looks at the mirror. She looks at him. Seconds pass.

"Come to bed."

Eyes shift. His meet hers. He nods and she pads away on bare feet. The image of his own eyes in the mirror lingers long after he's broken away. Somewhere a stranger shouts. Samuel washes his hands without knowing why.

8. Now

Glass crunches underfoot like gravel. Windows are out all across the building's front. The door is shattered, a hole. Glass pebbles twinkle under lights all down the hall. A ring of keys wait on the counter where mugs now broken and scattered once sat stacked or in rows. Carl's keys. Carl is not here. No one is here. A coffeepot bubbles behind the counter, ignorant of any change at all. No phone rings, no siren howls. Traffic streams by outside. Samuel pushes a button by the elevator and waits. The doors open. A song plays.

Upstairs. James sits behind his desk, staring out at the hallway as the elevator doors part and spill Samuel into view. Doors stand closed on all sides against whatever doom stalked these halls. If workers remain in this place they stay silent, give away nothing of their presence. James waits, all the fabricated charm now absent from his features. Slouched in seat, pooled, limbs hanging. Samuel stops in the doorway. James points to a chair. Samuel sits. The cushion sighs.

"Tell me about the devil."

"What?"

"The devil, Sam."

"That's not a question."

He asks what Samuel believes in. He calls him Sam, only Sam. He talks of God, of gods. He slaps the flat of a hand on the desk and demands the heads of trespassers new and old. He doesn't say what happened, or if he does it's lost in a sweeping, unfocused rant, spouting all manner of heathen blasphemy as Samuel only nods. He sweats, James does. Beads of moisture stand out on lip, on forehead. His rant goes on and then it doesn't, the words falling off and leaving behind uneasy contemplation. James watches Samuel, his eyes move and judge.

"You weren't here. Where were you?"

"James."

James opens his mouth to speak but he shakes his head and whatever word exists unformed in that mouth is gone, replaced with a grunt as he yanks hard on a drawer. The desk holds on. A scream of things gone wrong as desk drags across floor. Six inches, more. Samuel rises. The drawer gives in with a gasp. James reaches in. Samuel is already moving. A rock holds paper in place, heavy and smooth. He's grabbing, he's swinging. It connects with a dull thump. James' head falls to the desk.

He doesn't blink and he doesn't move. He doesn't breathe. The crown of his skull is dented and wrong. Blood pools. Samuel pushes the drawer closed.

———

Nothing comes out of the air conditioner. An ominous groan stirs behind gaping vents but the air does not move. The cab's engine hums, churns. Samuel spins the dial but the radio has nothing new to say. Floor mats once plush are now packed or worn. Glass pebbles sparkle. The passenger window is still gone and holes punched in door by bullets whistle in breeze. A rip runs along the vinyl of one seatback, from gunfire or not. An ambiguous light in the dash warns of some looming fate.

The body ruins the backseat. Fluids leak and stain. Limbs jostle with the motion of the car and fall still as Samuel pulls to a stop at the urgent swing of patrol car lights at his back.

The wait is long. A spotlight tags the car and doesn't let go. The world behind is bright while all ahead is only shadow. The gun in his coat is heavy and some primal insistence tugs, yearns to draw and call upon one end or another. He touches the radio dial. A pop song plays.

A dark form crosses the light. Boots thump pavement. The thick trunk of a uniformed man stops outside the unbroken cab window. Samuel cranks the gear that lowers glass. The man leans low.

"What did that solve?"

The voice is a wheeze, a gust of air holding onto thin words. Wide eyes swirl with a nameless darkness. The man in white stares out of the broken husk of a stranger's face.

"Not a thing," says Samuel.

The officer's mouth curls with the man in white's mad grin. "You're learning."

———

Walk. That's what he was told. Get out, go. Walk. The man in white said nothing of the cab, nothing of the body. Only walk. And he does. Samuel moves alone again in the vague direction of home, accustomed now to the turns of the maze, not wowed by the familiar twists, each one blunt and ignorant of reason.

His building. A man sits out front in a plastic chair. He takes noisy sips from a wide mug and he watches cars pass. Thick glasses hide the man's eyes and Samuel does not get close.

The building is a dead thing, all its tremors and knocks now gone quiet. He pauses outside his own door and without those footfalls there is nothing. He goes in.

Every light is on and the shadows overlap in that conflict, each echo of some object thrown this way or that, demented and wrong. Samuel is alone and as he falls asleep those shadows do not change.

———

The steamer emits an industrial moan that can be heard from the street. A little man in goggles pushes the bulky contraption to the end of the hall and back again. Tape holds new windows in place where the glass man did his work. Chemical scent clouds the air. Bleach and lemon and something else, something floral.

The regulars mill around the lobby, the offices. They take calls and nothing happens. Carl is distant, his eyes thick, pupils wide. He's changed his meds. He talks to the barista but the steamer eats his words. Samuel says nothing.

A man comes, a thin figure with round glasses that sit on a narrow face. He carries with him a briefcase and he takes the elevator up without speaking to anyone. No one sees him leave.

The following day the banks of phones that peddle bibles to the innocent and the soul hungry are gone. Wires protrude from hubs and end in nothing, go nowhere. The room is a skeletal thing, the remains of some nightmare organism. An EXIT sign glows with vestigial life.

The fanatics arrive after that.

———

Mister Kirby is a charmer. He glad-hands the regulars and he laughs at their jokes and he takes his coffee soft, cream and sugar and mint and more. He wears a tie under a sweater and he gives a knowing nod at Samuel in his coat, as if their ignorance of the day's heat is some shared secret, a covenant that is theirs alone. Mister Kirby exists in an aura of feigned, unsettling charm.

Casper Hill is next. He brings with him the stink of old sweat, ripe and intense. His suit is off the rack and wrinkled, maybe slept in. He touches the cannon tucked under his arm for comfort and he speaks to no one.

Burgess' guys. Carpetbaggers with guns. Fanatics and psychopaths basking in the Light of the Lord.

The regulars peel away one by one. Soon it is only Carl, alone in cold stoicism, at peace with the coming horror.

9. Then

The overhead light was off in Alex's office and a halfhearted lamp touched the room, its efforts soaked up and lost by the dark in every direction. It was another year, years ago.

Alex hummed and he sang. The words were not English when there were words at all. He yawned in his seat but he did not fall. He slurred his words. Dark glasses hid his eyes.

Samuel stood in the doorway unnoticed for minutes. He tracked all the moments that led to that time, that place, that moment, but he lost track, could not follow the thought. His eyes never moved from the gun on the desk.

"Everything okay here?"

Alex's song stopped. He turned in his chair with a wild swoop.

"Samuel. Yes. Sit."

He sat, Samuel did, and he waited. The humming returned and stopped, became talk.

"You know what this is. You know what they are."

He stopped and looked around, found his place, continued.

"A man once ran into one of them. Not like the others. An anomaly. A monster that lived behind a person's eyes. The man was so afraid of this thing that he took a knife and he carved his own face. His eyes. This thing scared him so badly that he mangled himself to keep it out."

"Did it work?"

Alex offered a pitiful shake of the head.

"He never did say."

10. Now

Her number has changed. He dials and hangs up and dials again, but the call goes nowhere. He doesn't ask Honest for a way to find her. He doesn't ask anyone. Days go by and then she is there.

The lights are off. He can hear her in the dark, the pull of each soft breath. He closes the door. He has questions he doesn't ask and ones he himself understands in only the vaguest of ways. He doesn't try.

They fuck in the dark. He says her name and she says yes and this is all that is said. She points a gun at him as he sleeps. When he wakes up she is already gone.

11. Then

The phone didn't ring. No one had called all day. Samuel sat and he waited but he was alone in the office, no calls, no Alex. The inner office was locked and dark.

A bottle left forgotten in a cabinet sat waiting behind cereal, behind cans. The label was foreign. Samuel took a drink. Expensive, smooth. A hand spun round and round on the face of a clock carved from the old wood of a forest long dead. He took a drink and he took another and somewhere a radio played behind walls, a song felt more than heard. The day slipped away but there was no sun in that place and he did not see. He took a drink and he felt the rhythm and pulse of a song that belonged to someone else.

He woke up with his face on a desk. There was a knock and a bang and men moved all about. Movers had come to take what mattered to a new place, a new office. Samuel rode along. No one mentioned Alex.

12. Now

The street preacher is gone. A boy hands out flyers for an accountant's services where before the cleric offered absolution.

"Where is the blind man?"

The boy slaps a handbill into the chest of a passerby. He speaks to Samuel without stopping or turning.

"Is that a riddle?"

The bank building penthouse is barren, now stripped of all its decay. The walls are a cream shade like soft skin but there is no smell of paint. The room smells like nothing at all.

The man in white exists alone in that newborn world. He looks out through pristine windows at what lies beyond. He doesn't acknowledge Samuel for minutes.

And then he does.

"Back for more?"

His voice is polite and fake, the speech of a thing without place, utterly without accent, a voice belonging nowhere.

"I thought maybe I'd come across Lou Henry in this place."

The man in white turns. He looks out of eyes like ink, a profound well of unfathomable black that envelopes the orb entire. Movement stirs in that void, something impossible to look into for long, a pulling, inviting horror within the swirling deep of those eyes. He exhales corruption. The grin is there.

"Is that what you want?"

And those eyes go on yawning, the will holding sway over that sea of black threatening to burst and run down pale face, to spread and drown all in that unspeakable dark. He turns away. Samuel breathes.

Taller buildings blot out the world outside the window. Fragments of more peek through, slivers of those places and their peoples visible in the fractured spaces left clear. Light dies above, only a pallid remnant makes it this far down. From where he stands Samuel sees neither sky nor ground.

———

Fever and the wandering lines of infection following veins have faded, replaced by a gray pallor. Skin hangs. Ever has lost weight, who knows how much. Not skeletal, not yet. A rag yellowed by bodily horror hides the ruin of his eye. He attempts but fails to fill the seat behind what once was James' desk. More clothes than flesh now. His beard is a wild thing.

"Don't look for answers. There is nothing profound here. We plug holes. Solutions are for other people."

He speaks in a whisper, a rasp. Pauses fall between thoughts. He breathes in those moments, the dead spots between things.

"Do you want to keep doing this work?"

"Are you in charge now?"

Ever shakes his head and cringes or grins and he shakes it again.

"There are devils all around us. I'm putting things in order."

"You're talking like a believer."

"We are being judged by someone. After awhile it doesn't matter who."

"Well," says Samuel.

Downstairs. Elevator doors open and the tempest is there. The apostle is blooded and swollen and he's dragged by the clenched fist of Mister Kirby. The apostle stumbles. Kirby seems not to notice. Smiling and beaming and saying pleasant things. Tie tucked between dress shirt buttons. Kirby excuses himself and he slams a door on the world, his prize carted off to its inevitable end.

———

Carl touches the radio dial. A station comes in stronger under that touch. He speaks into the mirror.

"Anything you want to hear?"

"Just turn it off."

Carl scoffs. He spins the dial until an old song plays.

"I got a new doctor," he says.

Samuel doesn't reply. Hands touch seat, scratch with a nail, but the fabric feels clean and the blood is gone.

Song after song goes by as the hours fall off. They sit watching a downtown office tucked in among dentists and one oblique door that proclaims only CLOSED. The world moves by, unmoved by their vigil. The car stinks of exhaust and the bitter twang of hot asphalt and the men only sit, wait. Every song is familiar now.

A parade comes along, a pitiful gathering of floats celebrating some unspoken event. Strangers march in wooden masks. A crowd gathers first to jeer and then to clap, overcome by the spectacle. Carved monstrosities stare at those they pass. Music blares and then passes. A pasty specter waits in the crowd, watching the watchers in the car from under a hooded sweatshirt. If Carl sees he does not say, and Samuel doesn't see at all.

Lou Henry carries a bag. Grease stains the side. He puts the bag in clinched teeth as he digs in a pocket and he is standing this way still as Carl steps out of the car, revolver in hand.

"Hello, Lou."

Lou Henry doesn't run, doesn't move at all. He looks at his keys and at the men and his body loosens. He may faint but he doesn't.

They move through a set of doors into an empty office space. Blue carpet, the faint smell of mildew. A door is set into one wall. Lou Henry sets down the bag of food. He opens the inner door because there is nothing else to do.

There are no windows, no places to go. Lou Henry speaks meaningless words and he reaches for a coat and whatever death hides beneath. Samuel hits him with the face of his gun. Lou Henry gasps. He drops the coat.

"Get up."

Samuel says it and when Lou Henry doesn't move fast enough he says it again. Lou Henry makes it to his knees, starts to rise further, falters. He sinks and stays.

The apostles notebook sits on a chair. Carl picks it up. He eyes passages with a lucid disinterest. Samuel looks at the man kneeled before him. He waits for some divine guidance to show him the way.

"I didn't do this."

"It doesn't matter," says Samuel.

A ceiling of cloud hides the world from the scrutiny of the heavens above. It isn't raining but it will. The air smells wet and clean.

Tables are bolted to pavement. Outdoor cafe. Carl flips through page after page of the apostle's notebook. He says little of what he finds there. He grunts, sometimes he laughs. He shakes his head.

"What a fucking lunatic."

He reads and he sips from a straw, something sugary. Samuel sits across from him. He watches people moving, vibrating, existing all around, an unbroken chain that goes on for miles. A car honks in a parking garage across the street. Packed wall to wall with steel or fiberglass, empty machines, their hearts moving all about, filling the streets, the sidewalks. They enter drugstores, they enter bodegas. Everything is too bright in store windows, buzzing lights casting the faces inside in pale madness. They stare out at the shadowed world, each unblinking, haunted. Samuel lights a cigarette.

"Hey."

Some kid, maybe fifteen. Keen eyes clock the two goons at the table. He decides they're okay.

"Can I get one of those?"

Samuel shakes out a cigarette. He shakes out another and hands over the rest.

"Take the pack."

Pleasing metal clank as the kid snaps open an ancient lighter and leans into flame.

"Thanks, man," says the kid, pale blue smoke leaking from nose, from mouth. A rain begins to fall. The day's heat shatters as a cool breeze crosses skin. Samuel breathes smoke.

RETURN POLICY

SAMUEL

"Twenty-seven bucks."

The cashier has a terrible haircut, curly and huge. Horshack on meth. He scratches his neck and pushes the paper bag across the counter. I drag the bag and the bottle of whiskey inside off the counter and out of the store. That side of my body hangs a little closer to the floor, just one more albatross I don't even notice.

A cab stops at the curb. A fat ghost laughing out an open window. The smell of old food wafting. A hand slaps at the door and more laughter. I think I'll walk.

Home is in front of me in less time than it should take. My mind is wandering or worse. The parking lot is full of huge boats of cars, long steel bodies made old and mean the way a car is supposed to be. It's afternoon. The sky is black. A curly-haired teenager in a skintight t-shirt leans into the open window of the smallest car in the lot. His belt is lined with bullets but he hates people who own guns. I don't know if this is ironic or stupid. He hands a tiny baggy to a silhouette in the car. Heroin and Tylenol. Cash disappears into the hip pocket of jeans too tight to be comfortable. He walks away nervously. The out-of-place car drives away.

Two skinny kids kick a soccer ball between parked monoliths. The ball is a checked black and orange. The color of Halloween. I turn to the kid who doesn't look away as I pass.

"What month is it?"

He doesn't grab the ball as it rolls under a Dodge built a lifetime ago.

"*Dónde está su alma?*"

He turns away as the other child crawls under the car to get the ball, tiny bird legs sticking out between worn and muddy tires. One hand in my pocket as I walk away.

The office. A bulletproof window is unlatched and open. The little room inside is bereft of the stationary figures who belong to it. A gray radio sits by a dead plant on a plastic shelf, words coming out but the volume is too low to be anything but distant hints at voice.

I lean through the open window but there's no one hiding inside, cowering in a corner awaiting the end. The room is just a room.

The foyer between two buildings takes me by an unplugged coke machine. A sweaty man plugs quarters into the machine in those brief moments when he isn't shaking. He looks at me and mouths something. I walk on without giving him any quarters.

My apartment is locked. I put my key in the lock and turn. Nothing. I take the key out and put it back in. Nothing. Thick shades are drawn. The room is dark on the other side. I lean against the glass, look through cracks too small to matter. A fan turns inside. I see nothing else.

"You stealin' somethin'?"

The sweaty man stands next to me with hands shoved into the pockets of his khaki pants all the way to forearms stained with tattoos of a tic-tac-toe game. X won.

"Go away."

He looks me over like he's wondering if he can take me. Like a slab of something edible. The edge of a narrow pink tongue sticks out at the corner of his mouth as one eye squints.

"Guy in there hasn't been around for a couple days."

I look back at the crack in the shades. The fan twirls in lazy spins with no real place to go.

"What did you say?"

The other eye squints with the first one. His arms push deeper into his pockets. He says nothing.

"I need to get in there."

"Get a key."

"Got one."

Silence. Hands moving in pockets and sweat and nothing.

"Doesn't work. Lock's broken. Where's the manager?"

"What manager?"

My foot connects with my door and the thin layer of wood snaps. This isn't the first time I've kicked in a door. This isn't the first time someone's kicked in this door.

The light is out and there is a void in front of me. I can hear the fan turning but I can no longer see the turning blades. The sweaty man is saying something but he is already so far away.

I step into the darkness.

There are whispers of voice in the darkest corners and from somewhere the smell of a haunted memory. I take one more step and there is nothing but the hollow black. A noise like shouting and the sound of breaking glass. The crisp slap of an alcohol stink. I can't see myself in the black.

The sticky sound of melted rubber follows my footsteps with every lift of boot, that awful almost-ripping, like celery snapping in half. I lift one foot after the other and the sound is getting worse. By the time I find the light I won't have any shoes, flesh bubbling and molten rubber oozing between scorched toes.

A light music plays on the air, something like chimes or less, far away and insignificant. The voice swells minutely and words roll out over and over.

"This is all there is."

Over and over and I clench my jaw to find the voice is only me. The walls sweat in the dark and the stench of everything fills me with its insult. Rotten and still rotting. I squeeze fist in my pocket and squeeze my eyes shut against the darkness but it finds its way in. It always finds its way in.

The heat grabs me and shakes. I want to take off my coat but I don't. Crippling fear to lose anything forever in this place. The darkness curves around corners I don't see and I follow. The ground slants at a tilt and I feel myself slowly drifting down, in. I clench my jaw tighter.

The voice is no longer me.

Whispers of whispers, hairs tickling my cheeks and planting in my eardrums, a measure below tiny, hints at words brushing up against me in the dark.

And more.

Maybe fingers or maybe tree limbs, maybe the loose strings of a frayed curtain or maybe the precious breath of some wicked god touching but not grabbing, nothing more than wanting its presence to be known. As if I could know anything but. As if I could avoid that touch. As if there is anything else in this place but that. Its hint is a mallet smashing me flat, the lightning crack of its energy standing all my hair on edge.

There is nothing in this world but that god.

All eyes are upon that god.

And here I am. In the darkness of that god.

The light at the end of the tunnel is no light at all. That suggestion of dirty glow is nothing more than an insult to light. Firelight in the vacuum of ever. Clarified in that glow are vast cracks and valleys in the ruined surface of everything. Floor and ceiling and wall and wall and the eventual void ahead, broken into pieces and waiting for me to follow. My voice is a stranger's and the words are out. I cannot stop them.

"What is this place?"

From nowhere. From nothing. From in my head.

"You know this place."

And the whispers are hushed. The thick plops of dripping sweat or worse are silenced. Even the plastic rip of my shoes stepping from the hot ground falls quiet. No sound can survive under the thud of that soundless voice. It says nothing more and still no sound comes back, fear alone enough to hold the world down.

Almost.

A single hair plays along my essence and clutches my heart. A single whisper sings on in a heartbreaking tone somewhere in the dark. I swallow the lump in my throat and I'm running, at first away from the dark and from the nothing and then not away but to, to that voice or to the glow that's almost there and to something, anything at all.

I don't fall down. I don't trip and sprawl but I should. At the full-on sprint I should tumble and roll and rip open a hundred seeping wounds but I don't. I stop and I'm standing. I'm standing still a long time. So long I wonder if that's how it happens here. If maybe that's all I can do. That standing.

The smell isn't the distasteful stink of rot anymore. A pleasant lick of smell has come up to replace that offense. She's sunken into rock ground and black oily gristle grows from the wall and onto her arms as they are wrapped around her knees. If she had on any clothes they've long since rotted away. Her flesh has turned to paper, her eyes lost and forgotten in the black holes of her skull. Her mouth is a frown and the pulsing muscle wall spreads its slick grip as I watch for eons. Only the sweet smell of fresh cut grass is still her own. Only the memory of that smell hasn't been ruined by this place.

"Oh Maggie..."

The whispers of the dark have become words.

And she's saying...

"Please don't leave me alone."

And she's saying...

"I don't talk to God anymore."

———

Click.

The light comes on. There is a paper bag by my foot dark where it has soaked through. A crunch of glass like ice when I step a foot on the bag. The smell of whiskey everywhere. A shaky man drenched in sweat is standing in the doorway of my apartment with a single dirty finger on a smudged light switch with one screw missing. His other hand is in his pocket and moving with the shakes. I hope it's the shakes. He's looking at me with something like sudden recognition.

"Hey wait, is this your place?"

APOCALYPSE CONFIDENTIAL IS

Jacob Everett......................................*Publisher & Editor-in-Chief*

Brendan McCauley..*Deputy Publisher*

Hermes S. Thurston...*Deputy Publisher*

Max Thrax..*Managing Editor*

Tom Will..*Poetry Editor*

D.A. Wohler...*Fiction Editor*

Tully K..*Editor-at-Large*

Will Waltz...*Books Editor*

FORTHCOMING TITLES FROM APOCALYPSE CONFIDENTIAL

Pale Townie

by Tom Will

July 2023